CROSS ON THE WORD

*The greatest gift God ever gave me
was hunger to know Him.*

Christine List

This book is dedicated to Don Zolinski: musician, teacher, visionary, husband, Daddy of our girls, and to our daughter Lisa: intercessor, song-writer, shining student of Love, wife and mother of two sons, John and Beau.

Without you I would not be the person I am today. You taught me to forgive and to love. I miss you both everyday, but the day is coming when I will join you in Glory. Then we will talk about everything, our understanding and love complete forever in Christ Jesus.

CROSS ON THE WORD

CREDITS:
Cover: Alina Zolinski Doud, the author's daughter, designed the cover
using photos taken by the author in Florida, California and Yellowstone Park.

Technical Advisors: Dan Stauffer and C.J. Packard

Proof Readers: June Hulce, Debbie Povich, and the author

Midwife/Tweaker: Debbie Povich

Inspiration: Ruach Ha Kodesh

PRINTED BY: **TBF** GRAPHICS DIGITAL

Zechariah 10:11 *They'll sail through troubled seas, brush aside brash ocean waves. Roaring rivers will turn to a trickle...My people-oh, I'll make them strong...and they'll live My way. Message*

FROM THE AUTHOR

Cross on the Word is a picture of God's love, composed of glimpses from one woman's path. You'll find a broken heart poured out at the feet of Jesus, and then made whole, filled with joy, love, and hope for the future. This book is the contents of my new heart spilled out for you, and for Him.

Each meditation topic is a quilt-piece from my life, followed by a crossword study using the NIV version of the Bible. May you, my fellow Earth-traveler, be touched by God's healing love as you ponder the life stories. I hope you'll enjoy doing the crosswords as much as I enjoyed making them for you.

CONTENTS

Sometimes trying to understand why just breaks your brain.

The reason truth is stranger than fiction is because we demand fiction to "make sense". Reality often doesn't.

All crossword clues are from the NIV Bible.

OCEAN OF LOVE

If I had the strength to yell for help, no one would hear across the waves, so I lay my head down on the boogie board, and thought, *Lord, I know You're with, me but I need help. I don't see any lifeguards. Would You please send an angel?*

Hours earlier, I'd pushed the 40 inch Styrofoam boogie board deeper into the ocean at "Children's Beach", Kona, Hawaii, intent on joining a group of teenage girls on surf boards in the big waves. A sense of danger tugged my heart. I thought *No, Fear. I'm going out with the other girls. I didn't see any strong current warnings, and it's a gorgeous day.* I used the borrowed boogie board to keep myself afloat. The board was attached to my wrist with a Velcro band.

Outside the protective arm of rock shielding the cove where swimmers snorkel among the fish and sea turtles in the coral, I intended to stay close to the girls, but the fluid rolling of the sea was hypnotic. I could see the ocean of love in Jesus' eyes, and I was in that ocean, excited to be alive, thrilling in His love.

A large dark shape appeared as the waves rose and fell. Was it a whale? I swam toward it. Just a huge rock, my whale "mirage" took me 30 yards from the girls.

Beginning to tire, and thinking of lazing on the hot sand, I headed toward shore. After kicking for a few minutes, I'd moved in the opposite direction. Realizing I was caught in a current, I remembered reading to swim parallel to shore. At the same time, a man passed by on his surf board, and warned soberly, "Swim hard."

Although I kicked as hard as I could the treacherous rocks came closer. I prayed, "Father, I think I need an angel. Where are the life-guards?"

A handsome blond man appeared on a surfboard between me and the rocks. He encouraged me to swim harder. I asked him, "If I can't, what will happen to me?"

In answer, he moved his board in front of me, and said, "Grab my foot, and hang on." The waves took the raft, filled my mouth with sea water, and I lost his foot.

I choked, swallowed, struggled back on the board, and clutched his foot. Again, and again, the waves played their game.

A long-haired, bronzed man came out of a wave on an eight foot surfboard. "I'm the on-duty lifeguard. I'll take over." My first angel stayed as I got the boogie board on the end of the rescue board. The lifeguard pulled with his muscular shoulders and arms, and I kicked as hard as I could.

When cramps paralyzed my legs, I said, "I can't help you kick anymore."

He turned, smiled, and said, "Just relax. I'll get you back." "You must've gone out before the warning signs were posted. Those girls you followed are locals. They know the currents." A larger wave picked us up and tossed us. He looked back and said enthusiastically, "We caught that one!"

Then I relaxed, letting my legs dangle; the safe sandy beach slowly moved closer. Thankfulness overwhelmed me. Once again My Father revealed His wonderful love and faithful care of this weak little woman bobbing in the sea of life.

Psalm 63:8 *I follow close behind You, protected by Your strong right arm.* TLB

Father, how many times do I struggle, believing it's all up to me, while You are on the job? Working or resting, help me be aware that I am surrounded, buoyed, and protected in Your great ocean of love!

OCEAN OF LOVE

© Christine List

ACROSS

2 Prov 14:27 The fear of the Lord is a --- of life, turning a man from the snares of death

3 Ps 112:7 He will have no fear of --- news; his heart is steadfast, trusting in the Lord

4 Ps 33:18 But the eyes of the Lord are on those who fear Him, on those whose hope is in His unfailing ----

7 Prov 29:25 Rear of man will prove to be a ---, but whoever trusts in the Lord is kept safe

9 Jer 39:17 But I will rescue you on that day, --- the Lord; you will not be handed over to those you fear.

10 Is 41:10 I am with you; do not be ---

11 Lam 3:57 You came near when I --- You, and You said, "Do not fear."

15 Prov 22:4 --- and the fear of the Lord bring wealth and honor and life

16 Ps 34:9 Fear the Lord, you His saints, for those who fear Him --- nothing

17 Ps 27:1 The Lord is my light and my ---whom shall I fear?

DOWN

1 Ps 31:19 How great is Your ---, which You have stored up for those who fear You

5 Ps 147:11 the Lord --- in those who fear Him

6 Is 41:13 Do not fear; I will --- you

8 Ps 27:3 Though an --- besiege me, my heart will not fear

12 Ps 23:4 Even though I walk through the valley of the shadow of death, I will fear no ---

13 Job21:9 Their --- are safe and free from fear.

14 Ps 34:7 The --- of the Lord encamps around those who fear Him, and He delivers them

15 Ps 46:2 Therefore we will not fear, though the earth give way and the mountains fall into the --- of the sea

Solution on Page 65

HARVEST

In Hawaii, on a special education teaching assignment, I lived near the ocean. One day when the sky was cloudy, the water dull gray, I went to the beach. It wasn't an inviting beach day for tourists, so there was only one other person in the water, a young man. He called and motioned for me to join him.

When I got to his side in the water, I saw what he was excited about. A huge sea turtle was lazily nibbling inches from his feet. He was amazed that it was not afraid of him; he had to share it with someone, and I was the only one around.

Obviously, it was one of "those moments". Silently, I asked the Holy Spirit to give me bread for this stranger. Luke 11:5-8 says we can confidently ask for "bread" for another, and it will be given to us. I asked him if he knew Who made that wonderful turtle. He didn't have the slightest idea, so I told him about creation, and our Creator Who loves us so much. I explained the plan of salvation through the gift of His Son.

We talked a while about his studies. He was in college studying hotel management. After letting him know that he could decide to be born again whenever he was ready, I turned to walk away. He called after me, "I don't know how! How can I pray?"

Are there any sweeter words a Lover of Jesus could hear? Of course, I turned and led him in a sinner's prayer. I don't even remember his name, but neither of us will ever forget our divine appointment with a turtle and eternal destiny.

Have you had the joy of bringing people to Jesus? If not, you can. Just ask Him to lead you to people, and prepare their hearts. Then when you find yourself in a "situation", ask the Holy Spirit for His anointing and the key to this person's heart. Then say what comes to you. He'll do the rest.

If you don't know what you're doing, pray to the Father. James 1:5 (Message)

Father, how awesome it is to be part of Your plan! How wonderful it will be to be recognized by others in Heaven as the one who was willing to bring them in. Please give me more divine opportunities.

HARVEST

© Christine List

ACROSS

3 Joel 3:13 --- the sickle, for the harvest is ripe.

7 Gen 8:22 --- and harvest ... will never cease.

8 John 4:36 even now he harvests the crop for --- life.

11 Mat 13:39 the harvesters are ---.

13 Mat 9:38 ask the Lord of the ---

15 Rev 14:16 He who was seated on the --- swung His sickle

16 John 4:38 you have reaped the benefits of their ---.

17 Joel 3:12 there I will sit to --- al the nations

DOWN

1 John 4:35 the fields..are --- for harvest

2 Rev 14:16 the --- was harvested.

4 Mat 9:38 send out --- into His harvest field.

5 Jer 8:20 the harvest is ---

6 Mat 9:37 the harvest is ---

9 Mat 13:39 the harvest is the end of the ---

10 Rev 14:19 gathered its grapes ...into God's ---.

12 Mark 4:29 he puts the --- to it

14 John 4:36 the sower and reaper may be --- together.

Solution on Page 65

4

HEALED ON THE WAY

Walking in Kona, Hawaii is always an adventure. Usually the man they call "Ocean" will pass by. Scorpions have been seen in his long tangled beard. Locals say he's been homelessly, wordlessly part of Kona for years, one of the drug casualties.

Next to the Kona sidewalk are condo sales people with parrots, artists with fabulous paintings, jewelry, every kind of Asian food, and clothing shops full of brilliant color. At Kona Shaved Ice you can get strawberry ice slush on a cone with a scoop of coconut pineapple ice cream hidden inside. The backdrop for all the activity is the warm turquoise ocean. Waves washing, birds singing, Hawaiian music pouring out of open shops and foreign languages spoken by the tourists complete the exotic sensory feast.

One day I noticed a small kiosk with a sign reading "Titanium Rings". Never having heard of titanium before, I stopped at the counter. The owner/shopkeeper was playing lively music that made it impossible for me to stand still. I asked him, "What's your name? How can you stand still with this music?"

He answered,"I woke up this morning with a knot in my back. It hurts, and I can't move." When asked, he gave me permission to pray for him.

I explained, "Jesus prayed 'Your kingdom come. Your will be done on earth as it is in Heaven.' Nobody has back pain in Heaven, so I believe He wants to heal your back." After a simple prayer, something like 'Please honor the name of Your Son, and heal Chris', I visited with him, asking about his rings and family and stuff. Before leaving, I asked how's your back? He smiled surprised, and said it was all better.

Two weeks later I went by the titanium ring shop to say hello, and Chris said, "This week has been my worst week ever in Kona. My ear is infected. Stuff is coming up out of my lungs."

"Should I pray for you again?" In one step he was at the counter that separated us, his head and arms bowed on the counter, waiting for prayer. It would have been comical if it weren't for his desperation. There was a customer there, whom he ignored, so I prayed once again for our Father to heal.

After I said amen, the customer said, "I stole a ring while you had your eyes closed."

I said, "No, you didn't, because I don't close my eyes when I pray."

This is hazardous work I'm assigning you. You're going to be like sheep running through a wolf pack…be as cunning as a snake, inoffensive as a dove…And don't worry about what you'll say, or how you'll say it. The right words will be there; the Spirit of your Father will supply the words. Matthew 10:16&19 The Message

Father, please help me to care about people like Jesus did, and to keep my eyes open to what You want to do as I walk through this life. Hear my prayers for other, and answer them to the glory of Your Son.

HEALED ON THE WAY

© Christine List

ACROSS

5 Mt 24:30 ..the Son of man coming on the --- of the sky with power and great glory.

8 Acts 10:38 ..doing good and healing all who were under the power of the ---

12 1Chron 29:11 Yours, O Lord, is the ---and the power

13 Prov 24:5 A --- man has great power..

15 Ps 63:2 I have seen You in the --- and beheld Your power..

16 Zech 4:6 Not by -- nor by power, but by My Spirit..

17 Job 36:22 God is -- in His power

DOWN

1 Ps 68:34 God.. Whose power is in the ---

2 Mt 22:29 you do not know the --- or the power of God

3 Is 40:10 the Sovereign Lord --- with power..

4 Acts 1:8 you will -- power when the Holy Spirit comes on you

6 1Cor 12:9 My grace is --- for you

7 Ps 68:35 God gives power and strength to His --

9 Acts 4:33 With great power the apostles continued to ---

10 1Chron 29:12 In Your hands are --- and power

11 2 Chron 32:7 Do not be --- for there is a greater power with us

14 Luke 9:1 Jesus..gave them --- and authority

Solution on Page 66

6

JOY IN OBEDIENCE

A surprising phone call came from the principal Waimea Elementary School in Hawaii. She asked me to teach special education, as soon as I could get there! It was the same school where I helped the year before, doing a church retreat in the cafeteria.

I had planned to be in Hawaii for 3 winter months again, so I contacted the state board of education to ask about substitute teaching in Kona. It was then that the principal in Waimea saw my credentials and offered to hire me full-time. It was a dream assignment. A retired teacher offered affordable accommodations a half mile from the school, and the Hawaii Board of Ed would pay for my move. Convinced that His will was clearly taking me to Waimea, I packed and flew out 2 weeks later.

Months into my teaching assignment, I stood in a parking lot in Kona, aching to see my grandbabies. I asked, "If it is Your will for me to be here, give me an opportunity to lead someone to You." A few moments later, as my Honda pulled out of the parking lot, I noticed a college student-aged Chinese couple running after the car.

Sensing a "divine appointment", I asked them what they wanted. They begged to be taken to the Ross Dept store. The back seat was full of shelving, but they said. "No problem. We'll hold them in our laps." So, next stop... Ross Dept. Store.

As we rode, I began to talk about Jesus, who He is, and why He left Heaven to do for us what we could not do for ourselves. By the time we arrived at Ross, the young man wanted to pray to receive Christ. As he prayed the "sinner's prayer", his girl friend wept for joy.

She told me they were from Hong Kong, and she had been praying for her boyfriend to become a Christian. God answered her prayer, and mine. His joy flooded the banks of both our souls. Hers was the answer of several years' prayer for her friend. Mine was the joy of being assured I was in the right place, in the middle of His will.

Philippians 4:6 *Don't worry about anything; instead, pray about everything; tell God your needs and don't forget to thank Him for the answers.*

Dear Father, there is no greater joy than being "right" with You. Help me to watch and pray, and obey.

JOY IN OBEDIENCE

© Christine List

ACROSS

1 Heb 12:7-12 no discipline seems --- at the time, but painful

3 Phil 2:8 and became obedient to ---

5 Heb 12:12 --- your feeble arms and weak knees

8 Ti 3:1 --- to do whatever is good

9 Heb 5:8 He learned obedience from what He ---

12 Is 1:19 ---, you will eat the best of the land

13 Mt 16:24 take up his --- and follow Me

DOWN

1 Mt 7:26 hear these words and put them into ---

2 Rom 6:16 you are --- to the one whom you obey

4 Acts 5:29 we must obey God rather than---

6 Heb 12:7-12 endure --- as discipline

7 Heb 12:2 Jesus, the --- of our faith

10 Num 15:39 --- not after your own heart and your own eyes

11 Acts 5:29 We must obey God rather than ---

Solution on Page 66

ARE YOU LISTENING?

A routine phone call to an insurance agent located an ocean away turned into a divine appointment. Todd and I were having a typical conversation between a car insurance agent and client when the Holy Spirit nudged me to ask if anything was troubling him. Out of his bruised heart he revealed how much he missed his recently deceased grandfather, especially the man's wise counsel.

The words of the Holy Spirit poured out, "Your grandfather lived a good life, and loved the Lord, didn't he? You grandfather still loves you. The Bible says we are surrounded by a 'cloud of witnesses'. He wants you to know that the love and wisdom he gave you flowed from the heart of our loving Heavenly Father.

Your Father in Heaven wants to sit with you, listen to you, and give you all the wisdom you need. Father God loves you so much that He sent His Son to die a cruel death on a cross, pouring out His life's blood to remove your sin. You only need to ask Him, and He will cancel everything standing between you. Would you like to do that?"

Todd responded, "Yes, I would."

"I can lead you in a prayer. You can say the words after me. Dear God in Heaven, thank You for sending Your Son to die for me. Please cause His blood to take away all my sin. I need You. I give my life to You. Please be my Father and help me to know You." After prayer, he was silent for so long that I asked if he was still there.

Choking on emotion, he answered in awe, "I don't know what to say. I've never experienced anything like this before."

We sat in holy silence until he was ready to speak. He thanked me and we hung up after I encouraged him to find a church with loving people where Jesus is preached, and to read the Bible to know God better.

Only the Father knows who the Son is and only the Son knows who the Father is. The Son can introduce the Father to anyone he wants to. Luke 10:22 The Message

Holy Spirit, please give me special appointments to touch the lives of others. I trust You for the words and the love. Thank You for bringing me onboard to participate in Your work. Amen.

ARE YOU LISTENING?

© Christine List

ACROSS

4 Is 30:21 Your ears will hear a --- behind you saying, this is the way. Walk in it.

5 Rom 1:5 call people..to the obedience that comes from ---.

7 2John 6 and this is --: that we walk in obedience..

10 Prov 19:27 stop --- and you will stray from the words of knowledge

13 Mt 7:24 --- who hears these words of Mine and puts them into practice is .. a wise man

14 Rom 10:14 how can they hear without someone --- to them?

15 Ps 95:7 --if you hear His voice do not harden your hearts

16 Rev 14:12 obey God's commandments and remain faithful to ---

DOWN

1 Rom 10:17 --- comes from hearing the message

2 Jer 11:4 Obey Me and do --- I command you, and you will be My people.

3 Mt 19:17 If you want to enter --- obey the commandments.

6 James 1:5 If any of you lacks ---, he should ask God

8 IJohn 2:3 We know that we have come to --- Him if we obey His commands.

9 Luke 11:28 --- rather, are those who hear the word of God and obey it.

11 Prov 19:16 He who obeys instruction --- his life

12 James 1:19 Everyone should be -- to listen

Solution on Page 67

TURN AROUND

It was 1970, and Don and I were students when we met in Ann Arbor, Michigan. We traveled everywhere together in his VW bus. For my comfort, he removed the front passenger seat and installed an easy chair. When I got sick from drinking the water flowing through New York City Central Park, he brought chocolate and wine, and I got better. Don's guitar serenades made me feel peaceful, and when I was depressed, he let me cry.

We decided we'd tried everything else, and agreed we might as well do "the family thing". We were both from Saginaw, so we went back there for our wedding. All our money went for a Sony turn-table and big speakers. We were both OK with apple crates for tables and a second-hand mattress on the floor in our rented bungalow. Don took a minimum wage job in a metal shop.

Our first precious daughter, Alina, arrived before we'd been married a year. Not long after, Martha, my dear Jewish artist friend who was in our wedding, came from Ann Arbor to visit. She told me she believed that Yeshua is the Messiah. I didn't know what that meant, but my desire to "find truth" intensified. Martha went to live at Ruth Heflin's Pentecostal camp, where she fasted 40 days for me and some others she was praying for.

I never watched TV, but one lonely day, I turned it on. The words I heard changed me, and my family, forever. Billy Graham said, "Kneel right where you are, and ask Jesus to come into your heart."

I thought, never tried that, never heard of that. I always believed Jesus is the Son of God; I even believed I'd see Him in Heaven when I died. But I had no idea He was accessible to me here in this life.

I did as Billy suggested, and peace came over me. Immediately, I heard loud thoughts, "Nothing really happened; it merely reminded you of childhood." I believed this "logic" and rose to my feet, immediately forgetting the experience.

In Matthew 13:4, Jesus explained that the Word of God is seed. Sometimes a person's heart receives the Word with faith, but "the birds of the air" come to eat it. Often called "familiar spirits" these demonic beings sound so familiar to people's minds, that they think it's their own thoughts. I didn't know it yet, but there were many "familiar spirits" following me around. Their presence was invited by my involvement in the occult, astrology, hallucinogenic drugs, etc.

Rev. 3:20 *I stand at the door. I knock. If you hear Me call and open the door, I'll come right in…* (Message) Come in He did, and gave me the sensitivity to recognize evil in my house.

One night I woke to see a "ghost" standing in the corner of our bedroom. Terrified, I did what I was told in the cult meetings; I called angels. First, I called Michael. Nothing happened. Then I called Gabriel. Again, nothing. Going up the ladder of authority, I called Jesus Christ.

Immediately, a tall brilliant angel stood at the foot of the bed. In one hand he held a glowing cross; in the other was a sword. As he held the cross toward me, I was wrapped in a cocoon of peaceful light. A minute later, I saw the light of the angel recede in the sky, like a star. The evil being in the corner was gone.

I made Don put our mattress in the living room the next day, and went to a jewelry store to buy a cross necklace for protection. It happened, though, that as I looked at the crosses, I knew that wasn't the answer, so I went home without one. I learned later that it is His name, and faith in His name that gives us the victory.

Matthew 28:18 *I have been given all authority in heaven and earth…I am with you always, even to the end of the world.* TLB

Father, I'm so thankful for Jesus! He invaded this dark world to rescue me! Thank You for Your promise to come in and live with me when I invite You.

TURN AROUND

© Christine List

ACROSS

2 Is 50:9 who is he that --- me?

5 Is 53:10 the Lord makes His life a guilt ---

7 John 3:18 whoever --- in Him is not condemned

8 Rom 6:18 You have been set free from sin and have become --- to righteousness.

11 1John 4:15-17 ..we will have --- on the day of judgement..

13 Heb 10:22 having our --- sprinkled

14 Ps34:22 no one will condemn who takes --- in Him

16 John 3:17 God did not send His son into the world to condemn the ---

DOWN

1 Mark 16:16 --- does not believe will be condemned

2 Heb 10:22 --- us from a guilty conscience

3 Rom 3:24 justified --- by His grace

4 Eph 1:6 grace, which He has freely --- us in the One He loves.

6 Is 55:7 Let him turn to the Lord..for He will freely ---.

9 1John 3:19&20 God is greater than our ---

10 James 5:16 --- your sins to each other

12 Eph 3:12 ... we may approach God with ---

15 Is 6:7 your --- is taken away

16 Luke 6:37 Do not condemn and you --- not be condemned

Solution on Page 67

OVER THE TOP

Aware of an evil presence in my home, I called a man from the "peace" cult who was a drop-out from the Catholic priesthood. He agreed to help and went from room to room with a glass of water saying "galactic" things not taught in any Catholic school. After making the rounds with him, I knew nothing had left, and told him so. He was irritated and told me to go see some people who ran a "House of Prayer". He said they claimed to have God's power.

The next night I was at the door of the House of Prayer door, reading, "Pray Before Entering". I said, "Dear God, I'm coming in." My sweet baby girl Alina toddled beside me, one hand held mine, and the other her glass baby bottle. We entered the front room of a house with some folding chairs. There were about 7 people, one with a guitar, and a young man in a wheel chair. A middle-aged Hispanic couple was in charge.

I joined them in singing some songs about Jesus, feeling comfortable with His name. The man leading, Mike Villanueva, said some words like "Shamboleiakum in the name of Jesus." I thought another chant. I will not learn another chant. Then he said, "The Holy Spirit wants to come into you." So, silently, I thought, Holy Spirit come into me.

I was sitting in a chair, and began to feel woozy, like I was going into a trance. I thought, oh no, not here! I thought I should ask if I could lie down. Then the man said, "Everybody, stand up." So I dragged myself to my feet. The man said the odd words again and took my hands. As I stepped forward (my eyes closed) my legs wouldn't hold me up. The amazing thing was, as I fell backwards, someone gently caught me and lowered me to the floor.

My back on the carpet, it felt as though two powerful beings were playing tug of war with me in the middle. The inner conflict was painful. Someone said, "Say whatever comes to your mind." I said, "Jesus, give me peace!"

People were kneeling beside me on the floor. They took my hands and said, "Your sins are forgiven." Wonderful peace, the relief I'd been craving for years, washed through me. Then, something began to bubble in my belly, like water. It bubbled up through my chest to my chin and then sputtered out of my mouth like water from a hose left in the yard, full of air pockets and leaves.

When the spurting sounds stopped, out came what sounded like baby talk. I stood to my feet feeling like a city power generator. My mind said, "Stop that! You're embarrassing me." My spirit said, "I'll never stop." As I looked at the guy in the wheel chair, the words were sitting on my tongue, "Get up and walk." I refused to say them, thinking, what if he doesn't?

Back at the house that night, the Holy Spirit took me from room to room, showing me things, like the astrology calendar, saying, "Jesus doesn't like that." Everything He showed me was shredded into the trash, or burned in the utility sink.

Before all these events, I couldn't understand the Bible, but now I read it every chance I got to sit or stand still for a moment. My new language given by the Holy Spirit gave me joy and peace. When the phone rang I reminded myself, speak English. I danced and sang, worshipping God as I changed diapers, prepared food, and did the chores.

Knowing Jesus was the best thing that ever happened to me, and I wanted the world to know.

Do not drink too much wine…be filled instead, with the Holy Spirit, and controlled by Him. Ephesians 5:18 (TLB)

Father God, please fill me with Your Holy Spirit. I want to know You better than I know anyone else. Show me the joy of Your salvation.

OVER THE TOP

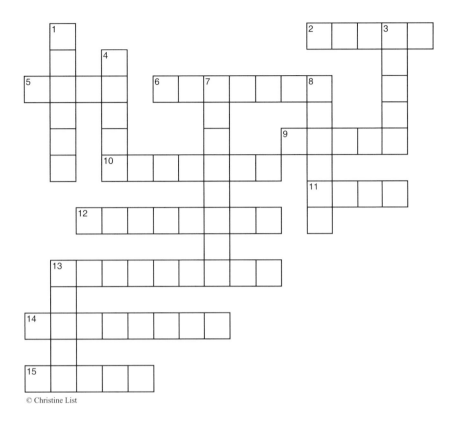

© Christine List

ACROSS

2 Ps 118:15 Shouts of joy and victory resound in the --- of the righteous

5 Luke 11:13 how much --- will your Father in heaven give the Holy Spirit to those who ask Him

6 Ps 43:4 God, my joy and my ---

9 Ps 92:4 I sing for joy at the works of Your ---

10 Acts 19:6 the Holy Spirit came on them, and they spoke in ---

11 Rom 8:26 We do not ---what we ought to pray for

12 Job 8:21 He will yet fill your mouth with ---

13 Ps 16:11 You will fill me with joy in Your presence, with eternal --- at Your right hand.

14 1Chron 16:27 strength and joy in His --- place.

15 Ps 47:1 shout to God with --- of joy.

DOWN

1 Rom 8:26 the Spirit Himself intercedes for us with --- that words cannot express

3 1Chron 16:33 Then the --- of the forest will sing, they will sing for joy before the Lord

4 Ps 4:7 You have filled my --- with greater joy

7 Job 8:21 He will yet fill your mouth with --- and your lips with shouts of joy.

8 Ps 28:7 My heart leaps for joy and I will give --- to Him in song.

13 Acts 1:7 you will receive --- when the Holy Spirit comes on you

Solution on Page 68

TEST OF FAITH

Friday was Don's poker night. One Friday I prayed "really hard" that he wouldn't go that night. I wanted him to stay home with me and our baby. We were sitting at the kitchen table, when suddenly Alina took a dive out of her high chair, landing on her head. Both Don and I were terrified. I prayed for my baby as her daddy held her, and saw her sitting in Jesus' lap, so I knew she'd be alright.

But Don didn't have faith yet, so he stayed home that night to watch over his baby. That was an answered prayer I never dared pray again.

Another Friday, we planned to spend the evening with family friends. Marjorie and her husband were in the process of moving to another state, so there were boxes standing in all the rooms. The husbands said Marjorie and I could go to the Full Gospel Businessmen's Fellowship International meeting, while they played pool and watched all the children.

When Marjorie and I returned hours later, the guys had just discovered 18 month old Alina sitting on the bathroom floor, eagerly eating and drinking the contents of the drug box. The men were scared and asked us if we should take Alina to the hospital. Immediately I remembered someone saying how painful it is to have the stomach pumped, and the scripture came to me, "If you drink any deadly thing, it will not harm you." "No weapon fashioned against you will prosper." So, we prayed for the baby, and committed her to the Lord for safe keeping.

As I watched over Alina in the night, she became hot. I brought her into the bed with me, and prayed the healing Word of God over her. All through the dark night, the devil told me I killed my baby. It was too late to pump her stomach now. Trembling inside, I stood against fear, quoting the words of life given by the Holy Spirit.

When Don woke in the morning, he asked how Alina was doing. I said she's fine, hoping he wouldn't notice how flushed and listless she was. Normally our little girl was a bundle of energy, babbling enthusiastically about everything. That morning she lay limp on my side of the bed.

Later in the morning, Alina didn't look any better. Don phoned from work and asked me to bring his lunch to him. I felt like I was really in trouble. The apple of her Daddy's eye would have to ride with me, and he would see how awful she looked. I put Alina in the car, still speaking healing over her. Suddenly she began her wonderful little chirpy description of everything she saw out the window. Our pint-sized tour guide was herself again, in time to see Daddy.

I prayed every day for my husband's salvation. Once as I prayed, a solemnity fell on me, and I "heard" the Lord ask me if I had to choose between Don's salvation and keeping him, what would my answer be? Immediately, I said Don's home in eternity was far more important than how many years he spent on earth. Over the years, I saw Don's life spared several times, from electrocution, falling from a ten-foot ladder to concrete, and the many times he drove home drunk from the bar without one accident.

2 Timothy 1:12 *I know the One in Whom I trust, and I am sure that He is able to safely guard all that I have given Him until the day of His return.* TLB

Father God, please help me to see my family from Your eternal perspective. I know You love my loved ones far more than I am able to love. I entrust them to You, in Jesus' name.

TEST OF FAITH

© Christine List

ACROSS

2 Rom 8:28 and we know that in all things, God works to the ---

4 Mt 9:29 according to your --- will it be done

8 Rom 8:30 those He predestined He also ---

9 1Pet 1:7 trials...have come so that your faith...may be proved ---

10 James 1:2 Consider it pure --- ... whenever you face trials of many kinds

11 Rom 11:20 you --- by faith

DOWN

1 Rom 8:37 we are more than --- through Him Who loved us

3 Mt 13:58 He did not do many miracles there because of their --- of faith

5 Mt 9:22 your faith has --- you

6 James 1:12 --- is the man who perseveres under trial

7 Rev 3:18 to buy from Me gold refined in the ---

Solution on Page 68

AND MY HOUSE

Rage and hatred blazed from my husband's eyes as he spit out, "Jesus little lamb! That's what you are! I'll take you to hell with me!" We stood by the white picket gate in the fence running from the house to the garage. Next to us stood the 2 foot marijuana plant Don had seeded beside my flowers. The once-thriving weed was now dead.

Looking him boldly in the eye, heart trembling, I said, "No, you won't, because God's word says that I will be saved, and my house!"

He liked his "old wife" better, the one who made powerful wine from blossoms gathered in the fields of Michigan. Not understanding the drastic change in me, he accused me of having a new "boyfriend", Jesus.

When Don was at work I spoke to the enemy of our souls to release my husband, spoke words of life over him, anointed his clothing, and his pillow. I danced with the Lord, shouted with joy for the glory of His presence. I poured out my devotion to Jesus, saying, "Whatever you want me to do…if You want me to go to India, I will."

In my spirit, I saw Don come in the kitchen door with a beer in his hand. The Spirit of God said, "Love him into the Kingdom, and one day when you stand before Me, I will say, 'Well done, good and faithful servant.'" From that day on, it was my quest to love my husband. Some days I had to ask many times, "I'm out of love. Give me more!"

Don was sure I killed the marijuana plant, and I told him truthfully I never touched it. What I didn't tell him was that I cursed it in the name of Jesus, commanding it to wither and die.

One night, as I worshipped Jesus in my bed, the wall dissolved in a dizzying sea of pulsating stars. At first I was frightened, but God's love reassured me as the familiar room disappeared. Taken to a measureless sea, I walked there on the sand, hand in hand with Jesus. Naked and unashamed, I looked at His face and saw the Man I had spent my life seeking. Perfect in every way, He is the Carpenter of the universe. There's nothing too difficult for Jesus.

Then He slipped behind me, and I saw on the beach a man getting ready to party with a 12-pack of beer. Jesus said *"I did not come to judge."*

I was accustomed to going to bed alone at night after putting our baby to bed. Don would come home some time after leaving the bar. One summer night I was wakened by Don's voice in the yard. I asked him through the window screen why he didn't come inside. He said he didn't want me to see him "like this."

"Don, do you want to stop drinking?"

Anguish in his voice, he prayed there on the grass, "Jesus, help me stop drinking!"

When I was pregnant with our second baby, Sarah, the Lord asked me to arrange Gray Hound buses to the Kathryn Kuhlman meeting in Ann Arbor. There were enough people to fill 3 buses. Don had no interest in going, but worried that I'd lose money, he came along. In the huge arena, when Kathryn gave an invitation to come to Jesus, Don left his seat and I watched him go forward for prayer, raise his hands, and return humming "Alleluia."

Don started playing his guitar again, and together we led church worship. A year later, the church went through a sifting, involving among other things, the pastor's son being convicted of a double murder. We left the church the night the pastor raged at us in the middle of a church service.

Weeks later, Don lost his job; Lisa was born, and Don started going to the bars again.

1 Corinthians 7:14 *For perhaps the husband who isn't a Christian may become a Christian with the help of his Christian wife.* TLB

Father, I leave the mysteries in Your hands. You make all things new in Your time.

AND MY HOUSE

© Christine List

ACROSS

1 Acts 16:31 Believe in the Lord Jesus, and you will be saved-you and your ---

5 Acts 16:15 she and the members of her household were ---

6 Luke 19:9 Today --- has come to this house

9 Mt 10:36 a man's --- will be the members of his own household

10 Josh 2:18 you have tied this --- cord in the window

11 Mt 21:19 'May you never bear fruit again'. Immediately the tree ---

12 Ex 12:13 the --- will be a sign for you on the houses where you are

13 1Cor 7:14 the --- husband has been sanctified through his wife

DOWN

2 Ex 12:23 the Lord...will see the blood...and He will not permit the --- to enter

3 Gen 19:12 anyone else in the city who --- to you

4 Heb 2:13 Jesus ...says 'Here am I and the--- God has given me.'

7 Josh 24:15 as for me and my household, we will --- the Lord

8 Gen 7:1 Go into the ark, you and your whole ---

11 Acts 16:34 he had come to believe in God-he and his --- family

Solution on Page 69

18

I AM GOD'S BELOVED

Pregnant "out to there" with our second baby, weary of changing and washing cloth diapers for the first baby, my body was screaming for hot fudge sundae and pizza. Several obstacles made my desires impossible to fulfill. There was not enough gas in the rust bucket car to go anywhere; and the money was gone until my husband's check came in 3 days. We had a wallet in the top dresser drawer where we kept the few dollars left after bills were paid. It was empty.

So, I did what any red-blooded American pregnant woman would do in my situation. Hubby arrived home from work to find me sobbing on the bed. After asking what was wrong, he asked if there was any money in the wallet. I told him it was empty. I'd already checked. He went to the dresser next to the bed and looked anyway. I saw him pull $7.00 out of the empty wallet! In those days, that was enough for a gallon of gas, ice cream, chocolate sauce, a frozen pizza, and a pack of disposable diapers at Krogers.

Once again, the Lord had showed me His love, in providing not only my needs, but also my desires.

Delight yourself in the Lord, and He will give you the desires of your heart. Psalm 37:4 NIV

Father, when things look bleak, please remind me to look to You, and wait for Your love to come through.

I AM GOD'S BELOVED

© Christine List

ACROSS

1 John 16:27 ...the Father Himself loves you --- you have loved Me and have believed that I came from God.

4 Luke 7:47 Therefore, I tell you, her many sins have been --- for she loved much.

5 Song 1:4 Let the King bring me into His ---.

7 Jer 31:3 I have --- you with lovingkindness.

10 John 14:21 He who loves me will be loved by My Father, and I too will love him and show --- to him.

11 Jer 2:2 I remember the --- of your youth, how as a bride you loved Me and followed Me through the desert..

12 Deut 33:12 Let the beloved of the Lord rest --- in Him, for He shields all day long..

13 Jude 1:1 To those who have been called, who are loved by God the father and --- by Jesus Christ

DOWN

2 Song 8:10 Thus I have become in His eyes like one bringing ---.

3 Eph 5:1 Be --- of God, therefore,as dearly loved children.

4 Rev 3:9 I will make them come and fall down at your --- and acknowledge that I have loved you.

6 Song 2:16 My love is --- and I am His

7 Song 8:5 Who is this coming up from the --- leaning on her Lover?

8 Song 2:3 Like an apple tree among the trees of the forest is my ---...I delight to sit in His shade, and His fruit is sweet to my taste.

9 John 3:16 For God so loved the --- that He gave his one and only Son..

Solution on Page 69

20

MORE THAN ENOUGH

Our babies were newborn, 18 months, and 4. Don and I went through some tight spots, and today was one of them. With no food in the house, there was nothing to feed our girls. I had no money. All I could do was pray.

When I got up from the floor, there was a knock on the door. Standing there with a big smile, and a bigger box, was a young man from the local butcher shop. He breezed past me and placed the full box on the kitchen table. "Wait, there's been a mistake! I have no money to pay for this."

His smile got even bigger as he said, "It's all taken care of." And he left.

Looking through the items, I found everything I needed: meat, eggs, flour, milk, butter, cheese, enough to last until my husband's pay check came.

Another time a family with 3 girls brought 3 huge garbage bags full of girls' clothes. Sweet dresses, play outfits, coats, etc. covered the kitchen floor a foot deep. There was enough to share with 2 other families!

The Christmas I had no money to buy anything for the girls, I knelt on the floor to pray. A knock came on the front door. Standing on the porch was a dear man from our church. He pulled 3 twenties out of his wallet and gave them to me to buy gifts for our daughters for Christmas.

Matthew 6:33 And if *God cares so wonderfully for flowers that are here today and gone tomorrow, won't He more surely care for you?* TLB

Father, looking back, I see countless times and ways of Your provision. I choose to trust You today and forever, to be my loving Father Who takes care of me.

MORE THAN ENOUGH

© Christine List

ACROSS

1 Heb 12:7-12 no discipline seems --- at the time, but painful

3 Phil 2:8 and became obedient to ---

5 Heb 12:12 --- your feeble arms and weak knees

8 Ti 3:1 --- to do whatever is good

9 Heb 5:8 He learned obedience from what He ---

12 Is 1:19 ---, you will eat the best of the land

13 Mt 16:24 take up his --- and follow Me

DOWN

1 Mt 7:26 hear these words and put them into ---

2 Rom 6:16 you are --- to the one whom you obey

4 Acts 5:29 we must obey God rather than---

6 Heb 12:7-12 endure --- as discipline

7 Heb 12:2 Jesus, the --- of our faith

10 Num 15:39 --- not after your own heart and your own eyes

11 Acts 5:29 We must obey God rather than ---

Solution on Page 70

SAFE HIDING PLACE

Michigan's ice storm, one of the worst in the state's history, came 8 days before the birth of our third child, Lisa. We lived in a hundred year old house with lots of windows, surrounded by big trees. The lights and furnace went out as power lines and poles snapped under the weight of ice. All night we heard the crash of limbs and trees.

My husband rushed from window to window with a flashlight. I followed him with the Bible open to Psalm 91, reading promises of protection aloud. Branches actually scraped against the house and windows as they fell, causing no damage! Thick silence wrapped us when everything was finished breaking and falling.

In the morning we woke to an icy white world. Trees, power and phone poles and wires made the streets impassable and dangerous. Our red Ford pickup stood unscathed in the driveway, surrounded by fallen trees.

On March 12, my folks took our two daughters, 4 years and 18 months old. I no sooner told Don that I was in labor, than he told me he was laid off from his job that day. Later, as I lay in the hospital with our beautiful baby girl, I asked the Lord, "How will You take care of us?"

His answer was the "silver lining" in the storm. Dad loaned Don a chain saw, so he was able to drive around town in his pickup and make more money cleaning tree debris than he would have earned on the job he lost.

He also had a miracle in the process. Standing on the branches in the truck, he didn't realize until he looked down that he was on a limb hanging far off the side of the truck bed. There was no support for the weight of his body and the branch, except the angel that surely held it.

Psalm 91:11 *For He orders His angels to protect you wherever you go. They will steady you with their hands to keep you from stumbling against the rocks on the trail.* TLB

Father God, when things around me fall apart, when it seems nature itself is against me, teach me to stand in faith on Your word. Help me to learn Your word before the storms come.

SAFE HIDING PLACE

© Christine List

ACROSS

1 Ps 4:8 You alone, O Lord, make me dwell in --

5 Ps 27:5 in the time of trouble He shall .. me

7 Is 54:17 No weapon forged against you will ....

8 Ps 91:9 -- you make the Most High your dwelling

10 Ps 91:14 Because he --- Me...I will rescue him

12 Deut. 33:27 The ..God is thy refuge

14 Ps 91:12 they will lift you up in their ---

15 Ps 91:7 A --- may fall at your side, but it will not come near you.

17 Ps 46:1God is our ... and strength, an ever-present help in trouble

DOWN

2 Ps 91:15 I will be with him in ---

3 Ps 84:4 Blessed are they who ... in thy house.

4 Ps 138:8 The Lord will ... His purpose for me

6 2Sam 22:31 He is a -- for all who take refuge in Him

9 Ps 91:11 He will command His --- concerning you to guard you

11 Ps 36:7 find refuge in the -- of Your wings

13 Ps 62:6 He ..is my rock and my salvation

14 Ps 32:7 you are my -- place

16 Ps 91:10 then no --- will befall you

Solution on Page 70

TRUST AND OBEY

As I balanced caring for our babies and home with reading the Bible, and prayer, my faith in God was growing. As I worshipped Him I "saw" a new car. My husband had gotten rid of the old one. He was concerned someone would fall out the rusted floor. Alina, our 3 year old, understood when I asked if she could see our new car in the drive. She had eyes of faith. Together we thanked Jesus for our new car.

I asked my husband what would be the best car for us, as if we had money to get one. He said a Buick Century station wagon. So, I went into the bedroom to ask, and thank the Lord for a Buick Century wagon. I sat in the driver's seat, seeing the yellow hood.

I didn't understand what God was setting up for us, but one Sunday, my heart filled with joy, I gave our last $20 until Friday in the offering. When my husband found out, he started packing to leave me. I went to our little bathroom, knelt at the "throne" and cried to the Lord. Later I found Don on his ladder painting the neighbor's house. I said I'd beg the pastor to give back the money. Sighing, Don said, "You can't help it. Never mind."

The next day Mom called and asked if I'd like to go for a ride to get out of the house. Knowing nothing of my prayers, she was going to the Buick dealership to look for a new car, and took me with her.

When a salesman approached me, I told him I was going to buy a yellow Buick Century station wagon for $7000. He did some checking, and the only yellow one in the state was loaded and higher priced. His face turned red as I said, "OK, it must not be my car, because my car is $7000" and turned to leave. He talked to the manager, and I got the yellow one at the Lord's price. When he asked me what down payment I'd make, the number $2000 popped into my head, so that's what I said, even though I had no idea where to get it. I had to bring in the money in 5 days.

Riding my bike around our neighborhood, with each pedal I said, "Help Lord! Where do I get $2000?" One of the biggest miracles ever, was when 2 relatives agreed to loan me the money. Two weeks later I was happily transporting my babies in style. The monthly payments for our car were provided by a home-based product distributorship that fell in my lap. In several months I signed up 150 people and had a thriving business.

If you will only let Me help you. If you will only obey, then I will make you rich! TLB

Father, please forgive me for ever thinking that You wouldn't take care of me. Help me to pay attention, hear Your instructions, and walk in faith from now on.

TRUST AND OBEY

© Christine List

ACROSS

2 1Cor 10:4 they drank from the spiritual --- that followed them

5 Ps 36:8 They --- on the abundance of Your house

6 Luke 22:30 you may eat and drink at My table in My ---

7 Mt 26:26 this is My ---

11 Is 55:1 Come, all who are ---

13 Prov 13:2 From the fruit of his --- a man enjoys good things

15 John 7:37 ..let him come to Me and ---

16 John 6:54 Whoever eats My ---

17 1Cor 11:25 This cup is the new ---

DOWN

1 Jer 15:16 When Your --- came, I ate them

3 Mt 6:25 do not --- about what you will eat or drink

4 Ps 36:8 You give them drink from Your river of ---

5 John 4:32 I have --- to eat that you know nothing about.

8 1Cor 10:21 you cannot drink the cup of the Lord and the cup of --- too

9 Is 1:19 If you are --- and obedient, you will eat the best

10 1Cor 10:4 that rock was ---

12 Ps 34:8 --- and see that the Lord is good

14 Ps 22:26 The --- will eat and be satisfied

Solution on Page 71

LOVE YOUR NEIGHBOR

The neighbor at the end of the street was a construction guy, a hard-working, hard-drinking chain smoker. A few days earlier his doctor told him he had throat cancer and would die in 2 months. In my kitchen, I thought of his plight. I'd never met him, only seen him from up the street. His wife had a hair salon in their home; I met her once. I couldn't shake the intense feelings of compassion I had for him. It was like being drawn to him by a passionate force field.

I prayed for him, but couldn't shake the urgent desperation from my heart. I called a Christian friend and asked her to pray for someone to lead him to Christ. She replied, "You have the burden for him. You need to go."

It wasn't easy to cross the street. I didn't know how I'd be received. At the ring of the doorbell, his wife came up from her shop in the basement. Her cheerful greeting was almost as if she expected me. I asked if I could speak with her husband and she led me to him. She returned to her customer downstairs.

Good, I thought, I can speak freely.

His appearance was shocking. He looked at me with bloodshot black-ringed hollow eyes. His breath came through a tube inserted in his throat. His fingers were black from years of nicotine stains. His once-strong body was shrunken and feeble.

There wasn't much call for ordinary polite conversation. His hands were shaking as he reached for a cigarette and match. Unable to connect the two, rasped would I help him. I have a strong dislike for cigarettes and the stench of smoke. Supernatural compassion rose within me, as Jesus moved me to lovingly light his cigarette and help him grip it in his fingers.

I told him of God's love for him. He listened. Never a church-going man, he needed to be filled in on some basics, but moments later he prayed for Jesus to save him from his sin.

Several weeks later the vicar from the neighboring Lutheran church contacted me. He had a phone call from the construction man's family asking him to come to the bedside of a dying man. The family never attended the church. It was simply the church nearest the house. The dying man was unable to communicate, so the vicar asked the Lord what to do. Psalm 23 was his answer, so he began to read aloud. When he got to "even though I walk through the valley of the shadow of death", the man breathed his last and left this world.

Even when the way goes through Death Valley, I'm not afraid when You walk at my side. Psalm 23:4 The Message

Father, when it comes to loving my neighbor, help me to do it Your way, speaking Your words in Your love, in Your time. Thank You for giving me the grace to cross the street.

LOVE YOUR NEIGHBOR

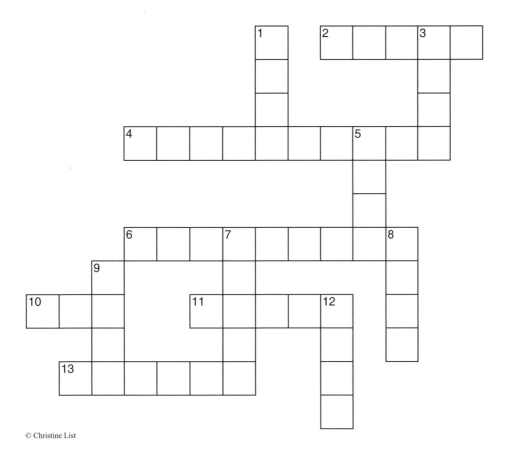

© Christine List

ACROSS

2 Ez 3:18 I will hold you accountable for his ---
4 Eph 4:25 each...must speak---to his neighbor
6 Acts 1:8 and you will be My ---
10 Luke 10:29 --- is my neighbor?
11 Ex 4:12 I will --- you what to say
13 Prov 27:10 better a neighbor ---

DOWN

1 Jn 15:12 love --- other
3 Jer 42:6 we will --- the Lord our God
5 Phil 2:16 hold out the word of ---
7 Prov 14:21 blessed is he who is kind to the ---
8 1Pet 4:8 love covers over a multitude of ---
9 Rom 13:9 --- your neighbor as yourself
12 Rom 13:10 love does no --- to its neighbor

Solution on Page 71

HE RENEWS MY SOUL

Each Christmas, the custom in our home had been to pile all 5 of us into the cab of the pickup and go to a tree farm. We'd choose trees and holler for everybody to see. Any less time than an hour at the farm would have been hasty. The correct tree would be tall enough to just barely scrape the 9 foot ceiling in our dining room. Its branches full and wide-spreading, the tree would occupy a large corner next to the window.

We savored the moments and analyzed the prospects until someone's feet got cold. Then we'd backtrack to the one we'd marked with a piece of twine, or we'd suddenly see just the right tree. All five of us would proclaim it to be the best ever and Daddy would crawl under the prickly branches and cut it down.

We each grabbed a branch and dragged it to the red pickup truck. As we paid at the gate, they gave us pop corn balls that got us all good and sticky in case we weren't already stuck to each other by pine sap. Singing carols, 3 daughters and I laughingly jostled for space between the stick shift and window. We returned home with our prize, where the next event would begin.

The tree was always too large for the old stand, so chunks were hacked out of the trunk until it could be jammed in, then my husband tied it with clothesline to a nail in the wall or a curtain rod to keep it from toppling. Lights carefully coiled and saved from the year before were optimistically removed from boxes under the stairway. They never worked at first try, so the lighting part was usually accompanied by my petitions for Divine aid, and frustrated expletives from hard-working Dad.

After the lights were up and running, then came the decorations. This was a combination of antiques from Polish and German grandparents. But the most priceless ornaments were the ones fashioned from paper, glue, used camera flashbulbs, glitter, and elementary enthusiasm. Faithfully stored year by year, they were stapled and wrinkled, but valued for the fact that our daughters made them. It took days to finish our masterpiece, but there it stood, lighted, garlanded with popped corn and cranberries, the most breath-takingly beautiful tree we'd ever seen… every year.

After the death of my husband, one by one our three girls married and left the house. I continued the tradition of live Christmas trees with college students from Taiwan and Japan who were living in my home. But that was years ago.

Now in a smaller house, all the students back in their home countries, living with a husband who did not appreciate stomping around a tree farm, I was faced with the logical, but unthinkable, prospect of buying an artificial tree. Realistic trees were too expensive; others looked like bottle brushes. The past sucked at my heart. My footsteps got heavier as I waded through dead dreams from store to store.

I saw myself in a barren landscape, alone under a dark heavy sky with no horizon. My dear friend and sister, Lynn, listened to my grief and prayed. Miraculously, the clouds began to part and blow away, freeing the sunshine behind them. Huge yellow drops fell from the sky, collecting in a pool. I soaked in the liquid sunshine of the Lord, as Lynn's living room became an infirmary of the Spirit. His anesthetic of peace pressed me into the couch and deep, healing sleep. Two hours later, I awoke feeling refreshed, alive. Weeping quiet tears hidden deep, my heart become whole again.

The next time I walked through an aisle of metal and plastic Christmas tree wannabes, my attention was grabbed by one different from all the others. It didn't try to fool anybody into believing it grew in the woods. Unabashed, its long soft fiber optic "needles" flickered in multi-colors. It was a perfect triangle shape and I loved it!

Pulsating colors, my new "tree" looked as happy beside the fireplace as I was to have it there. All the important ornaments and decorations fit the in spaces between the lights, and Christmas felt like home again.

2 Peter 1:19 *the light will dawn in your souls and Christ the Morning Star will shine in your hearts* TLB

Father, as my world changes, thank You for showing me the good things You send to take the place of other good things that pass on. Your love is the constant that keeps me.

HE RENEWS MY SOUL

© Christine List

ACROSS

2 1Cor 14:3 everyone who --- speaks to men for their strengthening, encouragement and comfort.

6 Is 12:1 --- have comforted me

8 2Cor 1:5 so also through Christ our comfort ---

11 Jer 31:13 I will turn their mourning into ---

12 Praise be to the God and --- of ...compassion and the God of all comfort

13 Ruth 2:13 You have --- me comfort

14 John 16:20 your --- will turn to joy

DOWN

1 Jer 31:13 I will give them comfort and --- instead of sorrow

3 Ps 23:4 Your rod and Your ---, they comfort me.

4 Is 51:3 The Lord will surely comfort Zion and will look with ---on all her ruins

5 2Cor 1:4 we can comfort those in any ---

7 Jer 8:18 O my --- in sorrow

9 Is 61:1 He has sent me to --- up the brokenhearted

10 Ps 119:76 May Your unfailing --- be my comfort

Solution on Page 72

EARLY MANSION

Our little house on Van Buren Street had no room for a vegetable garden, and Don had to crawl under the kitchen table to get to his seat. I started praying for a different house. A woman I knew from a prayer group called and said that she "heard" in her prayer time that Don and I should buy the house her church was selling to make room for a new building.

The house had to be moved; we knew nothing about house-moving; and we barely made our $135 mortgage payment, so the idea didn't sound good. But the Lord had a plan, and it began to unfold at the weekly prayer meeting with my friends. I "heard" the Lord say, "Claim the house." I asked Him, how do I know I'll like the house? He answered, "Don't you think I know what you like?"

Obediently, I said, "I claim the house in the name of Jesus."

As my friends prayed for me, the thought came to go look at the house, and if it had a Kitchen Aid dishwasher, and a built-in stove, it was the house for us. When I told Don, he agreed. We were amazed to see a Kitchen Aid dishwasher and a built-in stove when we entered the kitchen.

We walked through the entire 2000 sq ft house, brick with oak woodwork, 4 bedrooms, fireplace, everything we wanted, but knew we could never afford. As we stepped out the front door and onto the huge front porch, Don looked at me and said, "It's in God's hands."

The board at Bethlehem Lutheran Church was taking bids on the house. Don sat on our couch, and I went to the kitchen, saying, "God's going to give us a number. We'll compare what we heard, and that's our bid." I heard $150.00, so I asked Don what he got, and he said the number was too low. By then, I was about jumping up and down, "What did He say?"

"$150.00"

So, we made our bid, not even knowing where we'd get $150. Other people were also interested in our house. The wife of one of them had a dream and wouldn't allow him to bid. Another couldn't find a vacant lot. One found a lot, but the cost of moving lines was sky-high. At the end, people who wanted to dismantle the house actually bid ten times more than ours, but the church wanted to keep the house intact, so our bid was accepted!

The perfect vacant double lot was on the next street from where the house stood. Since the expressway ran beside the street, the power lines were high enough to allow passage. Neighbors tried for years to buy that property, but the owner refused to sell. The day I called, her dearest friend was dying in the hospital, so she decided to sell. (Her friend later recovered.)

Only one house-moving company was willing to move an all-brick building as large and heavy as ours. The bricks couldn't be removed, as there were no wood studs in the walls. We had to pay half of the move in advance, and sign a disclaimer that if the house fell apart, we were responsible.

We went to the bank to remortgage our house for the lot, and house-mover. The banker told us he was familiar with the house we wanted, and strongly opposed it. One of his other customers planned to buy and demolish it. I silently prayed while he told us every reason he would not give us the money, and then watched him write us a check!

An attorney friend gave me free advice not to take on the house, as we could go bankrupt. My parents gave us the same warning. But God encouraged us to keep moving forward.

The girls and I went to the work-site nearly every day. We took Saginaw bricks from the porch, chipped off mortar, and piled them for our new porch. Mr. Laracey, the boss, cautioned me several times not to be so excited, as the move was risky. Each time, I smiled and told him he was just doing the foot-work. Jesus would move the house just fine.

I made arrangements for telephone lines to be moved, and railroad crossing arms taken down for the house to pass. After months of preparation, raising the house on jacks and enormous beams, and digging a foundation on our property, the big day came. Excited to watch my home move down the street, I got the girls ready to go.

But the Lord said clearly, "Don't go." Mystified and disappointed, I obeyed and stayed home. An hour later, a friend called and said nobody knew why I wasn't there, but she was glad, because the railroad people didn't show up. Grown men were crying, and I missed the mess.

After rescheduling, the next attempt went smoothly. I was there to see two angels covering the house, with little bat-like creatures bouncing off their wings. A television crew was there to interview me. Tires on the huge flatbed carrying our house were popping like firecrackers. Mr. Laracey's smiling and waving son rode on the roof peak; kids and their teachers came out of Bethlehem school to watch the spectacle.

The crowd left after the house was set on its new foundation. Not one brick fell off our house; the chimney stood straight and solid. A wooden plank went over the big hole for the new porch to the front door. Mr. Laracey walked in and in a few minutes came back out looking confused. When I asked him what was wrong, he said, "The doors work! Doors never work when a building gets moved." I think the spotlight was on Jesus.

Later, as I sat in the living room, drinking in the beauty of the solid oak, high ceilings, and spacious rooms, I tearfully thanked God for giving me my heavenly mansion early.

Proverbs 3:5&6 ...*trust the Lord completely; don't ever trust yourself. In everything you do, put God first, and He will direct you and crown your efforts with success.* TLB

Father, I'm going to need Your help every day on this one. Forgive me for pride to think I can figure everything out. You alone know the future and how we are to proceed. Thank You for Your good plans.

Lisa serving at Heflin
Pentecostal Campground

Christine and Rae Ma

Don, Christine,
Alina, Sarah & Lisa

Sadie

New

Home

Early Mansion

EARLY MANSION

© Christine List

ACROSS

2 Jam 1:22 do what it ---
3 Jam 1:6 he who --- is like a wave of the sea
6 Jam 1:17 every good --- is from above, coming down from the Father of the heavenly lights
8 Mark 9:24 I do believe; help me overcome my ---
11 Is 26:7 the path of the righteous is ---
13 1Sam 15:22 to --- is better than sacrifice
14 Is 54:3 --- out to the right and to the left

DOWN

1 Ps 27:14 --- for the Lord
4 Jn 11:9 a man who walks by day will not ---
5 Jam 1:5 if any of you lacks ---, he should ask God
7 John 10:4 his sheep --- him because they know his voice
9 Is 54:2 --- the place of your tent
10 Josh 1:3 I will give you every place where you set your ---
12 Deut 30:20 listen to His --- and hold fast to Him

Solution on Page 72

STICK TOGETHER

Newly aware of Jesus' presence in my life, I joined the Saginaw Symphony Chorus to sing in Handel's Messiah. My love for Jesus knew no bounds, and everyone within ear-shot heard about it. Another soprano said her sister-in-law, Suzanne, was like me, and she thought we should meet.

I'd written Martha about my new relationship with Jesus. Her response arrived, urging me to get into "fellowship". As I read her letter, the phone rang. It was Suzanne. We met and have been growing together as prayer partners/dear friends/sisters for 36 years.

We met other stay-at-home mothers and began meeting in our homes each week for prayer. With our toddlers under foot, we learned the Bible, prayed for our families, pastors, and the nations. We learned to worship and enter the holy presence of God, how to listen to the Holy Spirit and share what we heard. It was in one of these meetings that Nancy said God would send me to the nations. As a young mother of three, living pay check to pay check, I didn't see how that could happen, but the word filled me with joy nonetheless.

Our problems were divided by our prayers, and victories multiplied in God's answers. Children got potty trained, went to high school, and moved away. Other women came to faith and joined us. Divorces and deaths happened, along with church splits. People moved away, and new ones came in. There's still a vibrant group of women standing together in prayer. When we meet, we start with the news: personal and world-wide. Then we worship the One, our King and soon-coming Groom. And we pray what we see on His heart, that His will would be done on Earth as it is in Heaven.

1John 1:7 *If we are living in the light of God's presence, just as Christ does, then we have wonderful fellowship and joy with each other, and the blood of Jesus His Son cleanses us from every sin.* TLB

Father, thank You for the "family plan" You gave us, for knitting our hearts together forever. Help us to be faithful in prayer for one another, forgiving every "ought" that comes up and, encouraging one another until the day we see You.

STICK TOGETHER

© Christine List

ACROSS

3 Rom 12:15 --- with those who mourn

5 Jn 13:34 you are My --- if you love one another

7 Rom 12:13 share with God's people who are in ---

9 1Cor 12:27 each one of you is a --- of it

10 1Jn 1:7 We have fellowship with one ---

12 1Jn 1:3 we have --- with one another

13 Jn 17:23 May they be brought to complete ---

15 Jn 13:14 wash one another's ---

DOWN

1 1Cor 12:13 we were all baptized by one Spirit into one body

2 Rom 12:13 Practice ---

4 Jn 17:21 that all of them may be ---

6 Rom 12:5 each member --- to all the others

8 Rom 12:16 Live in --- with one another

11 Prov 17:9 whoever --- the matter separates close friends

14 Deut 32:30 two put --- thousand to flight

Solution on Page 73

GLORY

I looked out the window of the airplane and saw a full circle rainbow. Many people go a lifetime without seeing the full rainbow. It gets cut off by the horizon and appears like a curve. But, here in the bright blue sky was the whole circle of pulsating color. However, what really caught my attention was the shadow of the plane. It made a perfect cross in the center of the rainbow. In that picture was a revelation about life and death.

Around the throne of God is a rainbow, the symbol of God's eternal covenant fully revealed in the death and resurrection of His Son. There's a circle of love, and it includes, but overwhelms, death. It's like the resurrection is the half of the rainbow hidden behind the horizon.

At 89 years of age, my Dad was diagnosed with ALS, Lou Gehrig's disease. He could still talk, with effort, and walk with assistance. He didn't want to go to a nursing home to be separated from his wife and home. A hospital bed was placed on one wall of the small living room. Next to it was a recliner where a neighbor, an experienced hospice worker, spent each night.

As a soldier in WW11 Dad's life was miraculously spared by the New Testament in his pocket and a roll down a hill after Japanese bayoneted and lost him in the dark. He spent the night applying pressure to wounds to stanch the blood while clinging to a root in the side of the hill. The Red Cross found him in the morning and after recovery, he returned to Mom with malaria and a body full of inch long scars.

With ALS, dad's prospects were grim, ending with a terrible death. Dad didn't have to say why he sent his hand gun back to Maine with my brother. He became morose, gloomy. Both Jim and I talked with Dad, reminding him of what he'd taught us as children, about our duty to God, and value of life. Dad made a conscious decision to honor God. There was no more complaining, and he became the sweetest man I ever knew.

On their 64th anniversary, I spent the night with Mom and Dad, made breakfast, and showed them the Bible verses God gave me for them. The three of us acknowledged God's sovereignty over death and life. Then we prayed that Dad's work would be finished, that the Lord would come for him ASAP, that he would go home at God's dictate, not any disease. The day of our commitment prayer, Dad raised one slack bony arm and waving widely with a grin, said "Bon voyage" as I left the house. What a brave, bold Daddy, I smiled through my tears in the driveway.

Several weeks later, in San Jose, on a mission trip, grief for Lisa swept over me, and I called on the Holy Spirit for His comfort. Instantly I "saw" Lisa, her Dad, and two children I knew to be Sarah's miscarried babies. They were excitedly planning a party because Grandpa was coming. The next day a nurse called on my cell phone to say Dad had been taken to hospice hospital by ambulance. Dad got his desired end one hour later; not one night was spent away from his wife. She'd held his hand and prayed with him as he fell asleep in comfort, 6 months earlier than medical predictions.

I was at the mall in San Jose when the call arrived. Glitzy, bright, people moving about… what a place to hear of my Dad's departing! A few tears, some unbelievably fitting words from strategically placed "strangers", and then powerful streams of party-time light/love/joy impacted me like waves from above.

Dad was on the upper floor of the mall, beaming at me, his "precious jewel". He wanted me to party, to celebrate. Turning, I saw a party dress store filled with pastels: mango, tangerine, lime, lemon. In my spiritual sight they swirled with joy at the celebration party Dad invited me to enjoy. I held a floor length ruffled lime chiffon in the mirror and saw my 60 year old face transformed in the beauty of Dad's eyes for me. A radiant, smiling young woman stood before me, dazzling at Daddy's coronation ball.

1Corinthians 2:9 …*no mere man has ever seen, heard or even imagined what wonderful things God has ready for those who love the Lord.* TLB

Holy God in Heaven, You show me Your glory in unexpected ways that give me joy and strength to live in this world while looking for the next. Open my eyes to see Your glory in every cross, victory in every death. Thank You. I love You.

GLORY

© Christine List

ACROSS

2 so that the Son may bring glory to the ---. John 14:13

4 Ex 40:35 the glory of the Lord --- the tabernacle.

7 Rom 2:7 To those who by persistence in doing good seek glory, honor, and ---

8 Those He --- He also glorified. Rom 8:30

10 Ex 15:11 --- in glory, working wonders

12 Ex 33:18 and Moses said --- show me Your glory.

14 Ps 69:30 glorify Him with ---

15 Eph 3:16 out of His glorious riches He may strengthen you with ---

16 Eph 1:18 the riches of His glorious inheritance in the ---

DOWN

1 John 1:14 we have seen His ---

3 and His place of --- will be glorious.

5 Is 6:3 the whole --- is full of His glory

6 John 11:40 If you --- you would see the glory of God

9 He comes to be --- in His holy people. 2Thes 1:10

11 Ex 24:16 and the glory of the Lord --- on Mount Sinai.

13 Ex 16:10 there was the glory of the Lord appearing in the ---

Solution on Page 73

FAITHFUL SAVIOR

Aunt Esther was diagnosed with pancreatic cancer in September, but the symptoms never went beyond some jaundice and loss of appetite for 4 months. I often wondered if she really had the disease. Her doctor was just as mystified. The tests showed it. I was visiting in the hospital room after her surgery for jaundice when the Lord directed me to anoint my dear aunt with oil and pray for her healing. That was in September.

Aunt Es was an executive secretary at Sugar Beet Products for many years. She was a decisive person, and no one could change her mind about anything. In February Aunt Es decided to go to hospice. She said she wanted to give up, to go there and wait for the Lord to come for her. She was still driving, lived alone, took care of herself, so it seemed premature, but her mind was made up. I was out of state for the first two weeks she was there, but talked to her by phone often. She complained there was nothing to do, nobody wanted to visit, she was the only one in the dining room, and maybe she went there too soon. While she was there waiting, Dad went to the hospice for one last precious loving visit. A week later, Dad was brought to the same hospital for literally the last hour of his life. He died before spending even the afternoon there.

After Dad died, Es complained because she thought she'd "get to go first". I told her she'd have to wait her turn. She laughed that after all, she was the baby of the family.

Two days after Dad's funeral, Es said she had a "weird dream". "The whole family died." Then she asked me, "What's it like to die anyway?" I'd found a picture of her looking happy and sassy, holding a fish she caught. I'd brought it with me that day.

"See the person in this picture? It's the same person, the real you inside. You'll never taste death, because Jesus died for you. He will come and take you by the hand and you'll go away with Him."

She smiled, relaxed, and said, "Jesus did it for me." We spent sweet time together. I felt so close to her as I smoothed wrinkles from her pajama top, closing a button that was open, and kissed her cheek. Cousins Dottie and Bob visited, and assured her that her taxes had been prepared. She was relieved that she found the 3cent error in her checking account, admitting with a sly grin that it was her mistake.

It seemed that she was wrapping up loose ends, so before leaving, I asked the nurse if Es seemed close to death. She assured me it was way too soon to be talking about that. Pancreatic cancer had lots farther to go before it would be done. But the Lord was into answering some prayers.

That evening my brother's wife, Henrietta, was setting the table, when an urgency came over her to go to Es. She and Jim went out the door, and the phone rang. It was Es's nurse. "She's taken a turn for the worse, you'd better come." By the time daughter Alina and I got there, Es was gone. The nurse showed me her own half cup of coffee, still warm, poured at the same time as Es's last cup of coffee.

Esther Martha, baby of the List family, was the last of the family to die, the same day as her dream.

1Corinthians 15:24 *Everybody dies in Adam; everybody comes alive in Christ. But we have to wait our turn: Christ is first, then those with him at his Coming, the grand consummation when, after crushing the opposition, he hands over his kingdom to God the Father. He won't let up until the last enemy is down-and the very last enemy is death!* The Message

Sweet Jesus, Your faithfulness in our time of greatest weakness is the greatest evidence of Your love we can know. Help us to see, and be thankful.

FAITHFUL SAVIOR

© Christine List

ACROSS

1 Heb 7:25 He is able to save --- those who come to God through Him

3 Ps 25:10 All the ways of the Lord are --- and faithful

6 Ps 33:4 He is faithful in --- He does

7 Ps 68:20 our God is a God Who saves

9 Deut 7:9 He is the --- God

10 Ps 145:18 The Lord is near to all who --- upon Him

12 Deut 32:4 a faithful God Who does no ---

13 Acts 2:21 --- who calls on the name of the Lord will be saved

DOWN

1 1Pet 4:19--- themselves to their faithful Creator

2 Heb 10:23 let us hold unswervingly to the hope we ---

4 1Cor 1:8 you will be --- on the day of our Lord Jesus Christ

5 Heb 2:9 by the grace of God He might taste --- for everyone

8 2Tim 2:13 He will remain faithful, for He cannot --- Himself.

11 2Tim 2:11 we will also --- with Him

Solution on Page 74

COMFORT

One of the best ways to get to know God is to experience Him as Comforter. Emotional pain can be debilitating. It grabs the heart, dulls the mind, and robs the future of hope.

My youngest daughter died at age 29. She left a husband and two baby boys. Even though she'd been sick a long time, I never thought she would die. It hit me so hard, I pressed my face into the carpet and made tormented sounds of anguish I'd never heard before.

Eleven months later came the first Christmas without her. She loved Christmas and chose gifts that showed her thoughtfulness and understanding of people. She had a gift for giving. The year before she died she gave her mountain bike to her neighbor who'd stolen her guitar, saying, "Mom, he never had a family that loved him like I did. So I gave him my bike so he would know that God loves him."

Christmas without her was unbearable. In a store during the holiday season, I saw a winter hat like the one that looked like our Scandinavian heritage with her blonde hair and green eyes. It was red with yarn braids on the sides and a pompon on top. My heart broke again, and I began crying uncontrollably. I tried to hide my face in the earring display until the sobs slowed.

Still choking on tears, I left the store and went to a prayer service at church. I sank to the floor at the front of the church, and immediately my spiritual eyes were opened. Jesus stood in front of me, smiling. He had His arm around Lisa, who was also smiling. He said, "It's OK, Mamma. I've got her."

I felt like a frantic mother who'd lost her child at the mall. I'd looked everywhere, and punished myself with thoughts of what I should have done to keep her safe. Then suddenly I learned that my child was safe with Daddy all the time. That's the comfort of the Lord. In one instant everything was OK.

Has the hurt ever returned? Yes. Even as I write these words the tears flow. So does the thankfulness, and the comfort. I've seen Lisa many times since then: Lisa dancing on gold, Lisa praying for me, Lisa comforting me. Each time the comfort went deeper, strength returning to my inner being. Each time the sadness is overcome in joy, the joy of His presence and knowing the beautiful forever holds Lisa in my future.

All praise to the God and Father of our Master, Jesus the Messiah! Father of all mercy! God of all healing counsel! He comes alongside us when we go through hard times, and before you know it, he brings us alongside someone else who is going through hard times so that we can be there for that person just as God was there for us. We have plenty of hard times that come from following the Messiah, but no more so than the good times of his healing comfort-we get a full measure of that, too.
2 Corinthians 1:3-7 The Message

Father, when my heart aches, I look to You to comfort me. Help me to be a comfort to others. Show us Your goodness in the land of the living.

COMFORT

© Christine List

ACROSS

4 Ps.71:21 You will increase my--- and comfort me once again.

8 Job16:5 comfort from my ---would bring you relief

9 Lam.1:2 Among all her ---there is none to comfort her

10 Job7:13 I think my bed will comfort me and my couch will ease my ---

11 Ruth 2:13 you have ---me comfort

12 Job36:16 He is wooing you from the ---of distress..to the comfort of you table

13 Is.66:13 As a mother comforts her child, so will I comfort you; and you will be comforted over ---

14 Gen.37:35 All his sons and daughters came to comfort him, but he ---to be comforted.

DOWN

1 Ps.119:50 My comfort in my suffering is this: Your ---preserves my life.

2 Luke6:24 But ---to you who are rich, for you have already received your comfort

3 Ps.119:52 I remember Your ---laws, o Lord, and I find comfort in them

5 2Cor1:4 Who comforts us in all our ---, so that we can comfort those in any trouble with the comfort we ourselves have received from God

6 2Cor1:6 If we are ---, it is for your comfort and salvation

7 2Cor2:7 Now instead, you ought to --- and comfort him, so that he will not be overwhelmed by excessive sorrow

Solution on Page 74

ANGELS IN THE MEADOW

The marriage I entered 7 years after Don died turned into a struggle for emotional and spiritual survival. Two weeks after our marriage I asked why he was looking at me in a strange way. He said, "I'm imagining what you'll look like in your casket." Then he smiled like a boy caught with his hand in the cookie jar.

In the face of hostility, anger, strife, verbal, and finally physical abuse, I took my stand to endure. I fasted, prayed, forgave, quoted every good promise I could find in the Bible. The most critical contest was to keep my heart free from bitterness, refuse to become the enemy.

I awoke one night with my husband standing at the side of the bed, his big strong hand on my neck. I couldn't see him in the dark, but felt him trembling with rage. Silent prayers shouted inside my head until he withdrew. There were moments of bliss, always followed by acts of terrorism, loud torrents of cursing rage.

For six years I refused to give up hope for the beautiful marriage I knew we could have.

One time, as I cried out to God that I couldn't take any more, a huge sunny meadow appeared. Angels walked there in the flowers. One angel came close and peered into my eyes. His eyes were blue pools with the sun sparkling. I wondered if he saw the weariness, wariness of a hunted animal. Could he see evidence of battles he'd never fight, or was he with me the entire time, playing a part in my survival?

Reflected in his face was cherishing love. Maybe I could safely lay down my weapons. Did I hold the dagger in my hand, or was it now a part of my hand, welded to the bone by hard opposition?

The truth dawned in my soul, the joy, peace, beauty in the meadow is real, and always mine, always available to me. It is my meadow, the safe place of His presence.

Psalm 23:5&6 *You serve me a six-course dinner right in front of my enemies. You revive my drooping head; my cup brims with blessing…I'm back home in the house of God for the rest of my life.* Message

Father God, deliver me from evil. Protect my heart. Don't let it turn to stone. Refresh me in Your safe place, and remind me that You love me. Teach me when to stand and when to leave. And when it's time to leave, show me the safe escape route.

ANGELS IN THE MEADOW

© Christine List

ACROSS

3 Ps 147:11 the Lord --- in those who fear Him, who put their hope in His unfailing love.

5 Jer 39:17 But I will rescue you on that day, --- the Lord; you will not be handed over to those you fear.

7 Prov 22:4 --- and the fear of the Lord bring wealth and honor and life.

10 Ps 23:4 Even though I walk through the valley of the shadow of death, I will fear no---..

11 Prov 29:25 Fear of man will prove to be a ---, but whoever trusts in the Lord is kept safe.

12 Ps 112:8 His heart is ---, he will have no fear; in the end he will look in triumph on his foes.

13 Ps 34:9 Fear the Lord, you His saints, for those who fear Him ---nothing.

14 Ps 34:7 The ---of the Lord encamps around those who fear Him, and He delivers them.

15 Is 33:6 He will be the sure ---for your times, a rich store of salvation and wisdom and knowledge; the fear of the Lord is the key to this treasure.

DOWN

1 Ps 46:2 Therefore we will not fear, though the earth give way and the mountains fall into the ---of the sea

2 Ps 112:10 He will have no fear of ---news; his heart is steadfast, trusting in the Lord.

4 Is 41:13 Do not fear; I will ---you.

6 Job 11:15 then you will lift up your face without ---; you will stand firm and without fear.

7 Luke 12:5 Fear Him Who..has power to throw you into ---.

8 Ps 3:6 I will not fear the tens of ---drawn up against me on every side.

9 Lam 3:57 You came near when I ---You, and You said, "Do not fear."

11 Ex 20:20 Do not be afraid. God has come to test you, so that the fear of God will be with you to keep you from ---.

Solution on Page 75

44

CHOOSE JOY

Did you ever get hit so hard that you felt like you couldn't go on? Two weeks after the unexpected death of my youngest daughter, my husband, angry that I wouldn't lie down on the front seat of his truck, grabbed my hair and smashed his powerful fist into my chest.

We were on our way to a friend's birthday party. Pieces of my hair spun around the brightly colored helium balloon like confetti in the cab of the truck. He drove back to the house and I sat in the driveway, calling people on my cell phone. I should have called the police, but was too embarrassed. My chest hurt and I couldn't sleep. Several days later a doctor confirmed that my sternum was pushed in, and ribs out of place.

I went to my husband's doctor hoping he'd tell me my husband was bipolar or had a tumor, something that could be fixed. He told me my husband is a "bully" and to talk to an abuse counselor and an attorney. The counselor helped me realize things were getting worse, not better. I'd already kept an over-night bag packed for quick escape from his rages. Realizing I didn't have the emotional strength to leave the marriage so shortly after the death of my daughter, she advised I stay safe and wait for my opportunity. Almost a year later, after more failed attempts at counseling, my husband left for a three month "nostalgia road trip" out west.

I was left behind with my terminally ill dad and his sister with pancreatic cancer. After Dad died, I talked to his pastor about my marriage, and he urged me to get out now. In the spirit I saw myself standing in a prison cell, with an open door. I heard the words, "The only one who can keep you inside is you." I stepped out, breathed freedom, and then agonized over whether it was right to leave a marriage. With the support of my mother, friends, daughters, pastor, neighbors, I stayed out. Since then, I read books about men who hate women and understand what I was caught in.

When it was time to look at myself in the mirror I didn't recognize myself. A frown had frozen on my once happy face. I wanted to smile again, but I couldn't. I remembered reading about a fashion model who suffered paralysis. She watched herself in the mirror, willing her muscles to perform. Trying her method, I pulled the corners of my mouth back as close as I could to my ears. A check in the mirror revealed a believable-looking smile. Reminding myself many times during the day to pull my lips back, I felt so silly that it made me laugh out loud.

Gradually the priceless revelation came. Joy, like salvation, is a free gift! It doesn't have to be "deserved" by having "good things" happen. Just as I'd made a decision to receive Jesus' salvation from sin, by faith I received His joy. *Happiness* depends on *circumstances*. I have the power to *choose* joy.

Like the model who willed her unresponsive legs to walk, I taught my face to be happy again. As I continue to praise God, and thank Him for His love, joy is a gift that bubbles from inside a heart where Jesus lives.

No one can force us to rebuild our identity around horrible events in our lives. As my Daddy used to say, "Everybody is about as happy as he decides to be." I decided, by my God-given will, to live with joy. The Holy Spirit has backed me up with the real deal.

The joy of the Lord is our strength. The Lord hasn't chosen for us to walk life's path struggling under load of grief any more than He called us to stumble under a load of sin.

*I place before you Life and Death, Blessing and Curse. Choose life so that you and your children will live. And love God, your God, listening obediently to him, firmly embracing him. Oh yes, he is life itself, a long life…*Deuteronomy 19&20 The Message

"*In this world you shall have tribulation, but be of good cheer, for I have overcome the world.*" John 16:33 KJV

Please say with me, "Father God, I choose joy even when it makes no sense. Please help me to honor You by receiving Your all-sufficient joy"

CHOOSE JOY

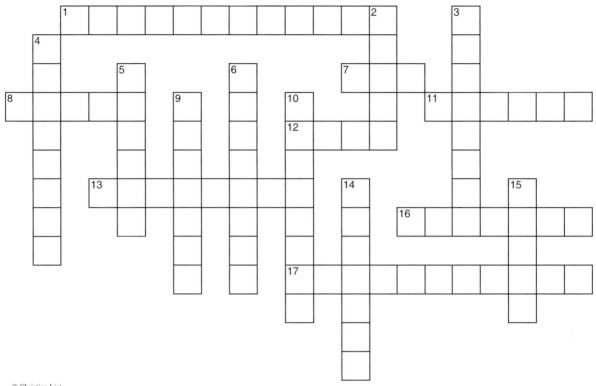

© Christine List

ACROSS

1 John 3:29 full of joy when he hears the --- voice

7 Ps 16:11 You will fill me with ---

8 Ps 48:2 the joy of the whole ---

11 Prov 12:14 from the fruit of his lips a man is --- with good things

12 1John 3:19&20 we set our hearts at ---

13 2Cor 7:4 in all our --- my joy knows no bounds

16 Ps 37:3&4 give you the ---of your heart

17 Ps 94:19 Your --- brought joy to my soul

DOWN

2 Is 26:19 wake up and --- for joy

3 Ps 36:7-9 drink from Your river of ---

4 Is 51:11 ---and joy will overtake them

5 Is 61:7 everlasting joy will be ---

6 John 15:11 that your joy may be---

9 Heb 12:2 for the joy set before Him--

10 Acts 2:28 You fill me with joy in Your ----

14 Ps 30:5 rejoicing comes in the ---

15 Gal 5:22 the --- of the Spirit is love, joy

Solution on Page 75

POWER OF FORGIVENESS

It was "wear your decorated rain bonnet" day at Lapeer, Michigan Curves. "Fran" was on the exercise machine next to me, her long red hair decked out in a bonnet covered with glued-on flowers. She turned to me to say, "I'm late today. I slept until 11. I took 3 sleeping pills from the doctor."

As we continued exercising, I asked the Holy Spirit what to say. The question came, "How come you're not sleeping at night?"

"I have too much stress in my life." Her eyes were glassy, and the smell of smoke traveled with her. She began to tell of her boss, and good benefits that kept her on a difficult job. She said she read the Bible and prayed for her boss. Remembering a lesson on Godly favor I'd read that morning, I began to share it with her.

"God promises to surround us with favor if we are believers in Christ Jesus. If we have problems, it could be due to unforgiveness in our lives." Her eyes shot open.

"That would be my grandparents!" As I pulled on the lat machine and she jogged in place, she continued the story of broken relationship and pain, then said, "I never heard of that before. It makes sense."

"If we think about what Jesus suffered for us, no one ever hurt us that bad. He wants us to give away the forgiveness He gave us. If they're dead, you can still tell them you're sorry for holding things against them, and let them off the hook."

As I finished my last machine, she said with a new smile on her face, "That's a good idea. I'm going to do that."

One day in the spotlight of the Holy Spirit, saw the cells "in the basement", below my conscious mind. People were imprisoned there. I opened the cell door, letting each go free with a written statement, "Forgiven". Then I asked the Lord for the grace to open my own cell, granting myself forgiveness.

There is no greater price than the blood of Jesus that can be paid for sin. If I demand someone to pay for their own sin, then I must also pay for mine. I can't even begin to do that. Only the blood of Jesus has the power to remove the pain of sin.

Matthew 6:15 *Your heavenly Father will forgive you if you forgive those who sin against you; but if you refuse to forgive them, He will not forgive you.* TLB

Search my heart, Lord, and show me if there's anyone I have not forgiven. I realize that my lack of forgiveness opens the door to satan to torment me. Thank You for Your power to forgive myself, as well as others.

POWER OF FORGIVENESS

© Christine List

ACROSS

2 Mt 18:21 Lord, how many times shall I forgive my ---

5 Mt 6:14 For ---you forgive men when they sin against you...

7 Luke 17:3 If your brother sins, --- him, and if he repents, forgive him.

9 Mk 11:25 if you hold --- against anyone, forgive him..

12 Col 3:13 forgive whatever --- you may have against one another.

13 Ps 86:5 You are forgiving and ---, O Lord

15 Mt 6:15 ..if you do not forgive... your Father will --- forgive your sins.

17 Eph 4:27 do not give the devil a ---

DOWN

1 2Cor 2:7 forgive and --- him

3 Luke 24:47 repentance and forgiveness of sins will be -- in His name

4 Mt 6:12 Forgive us...as we also have forgiven our ---

6 Luke 6:37 Forgive, and you will be ---.

8 Eph 4:32 Be --- and compassionate to one another, forgiving each other...

10 Col 2:13 He forgave us all our ---.

11 Ps 19:12 Forgive my --- faults.

14 2Cor 2:10-11 I have forgiven ..in order that satan might not --- us

16 Jer 33:8 I will... forgive --- their sins of rebellion

Solution on Page 76

GUILT FREE

Imagine coming into the presence of the King of kings. He is holy, more powerful than any being in the universe. With one word He can move a mountain, rock the earth, and dump the contents of the sea on a city. He has said, "Come unto Me", but I know the mistakes I've made. Worse, I remember the times I was deliberately cruel, times when my passive stupidity harmed others. How can I dare present myself before Him? It's more than my track record. It's who I am. If I am honest, I see that there is nothing good in me. Any good gift, any pleasantness, is a gift from Him.

All of the mess, fuss, disaster, destruction, and devastation in my life is due to sin, my own and others'. I know my dismal failure. How can I look at the face of God? Then I hear the Savior's tender voice calling me to Himself. I peek His way, and He's smiling. In His eyes, I see an ocean of love.

He is saying, "My darling, My love, I fought dragons for you. Everything that torments you came against Me. I absorbed all your guilt, your shame, your wandering from Truth. I let angry men nail Me to a tree, gave every drop of Heaven's life-blood to blot out every word recorded against you.

I gave My life for you, because I want you. You have believed a lie, that your value is linked to other's opinions of you. Not even your own assessment can be trusted. It was shaped by the world around you. I want you to see yourself as I see you: worth the death of the King. I died to win you from the dark pretender, to rescue you. I want you!

Why would I leave My home, My Father, the company of angels, to endure the cross and then turn My back on you? You were the point of it all. So come freely, and come often."

> *"Oh, get up, dear friend,*
>> *My fair and beautiful lover- come to Me!*
> *Come, my shy and modest dove-*
>> *leave your seclusion, come out in the open.*
> *Let Me see your face,*
>> *let Me hear your voice*
> *For your voice is soothing*
>> *and your face is ravishing. "* Song of Songs 2:14 The Message

Father God, when my heart condemns me, when the accuser's voice is loud in my ears, please help me to know You receive me for the sake of Your Son. Comfort my sin-sick heart with Your perfect love.

GUILT FREE

© Christine List

ACROSS

4 Ex.34:6 the Lord, the Lord, the compassionate and gracious God, slow to anger, --- in love and faithfulness

5 1Cor 13:12 I shall know ---

6 Ex.20:6 but showing love to a --- generations of those who love Me and keep My commandments

8 1Cor 4:5 He will expose the --- of men's hearts

11 Heb 10:22 having your hearts ---

12 Deut.7:12 the Lord your God will keep His --- of love with you

14 Rom 8:1 no condemnation for those who are --- Christ Jesus

15 1Cor 4:3 I do not even --- myself

16 Deut.6:5 Love the Lord your God with all your heart and with all your soul and with all your ---

DOWN

1 Ps 38:4 My --- has overwhelmed me

2 Is 6:7 your guilt is taken ---

3 Ex.15:13 In Your --- love You will lead the people You have redeemed. In Your strength You will guide them to Your holy dwelling.

7 Lev.19:18 love your --- as yourself

9 Rom 5:19 through the --- of the one man the many will be made righteous

10 Gen.29:20 So Jacob served --- years to get Rachel, but they seemed like only a few days to him because of his love for her

13 Deut.7:13 He will love you and bless you and increase your ---

Solution on Page 76

50

AUTHORITY

Anwar lurched to the side, as if struck by an unseen 2x4. The handsome young Saudi Arabian staggered, dropped into the couch, and with shaking hands lit a cigarette. "I have never heard this before!"

Anwar came to Saginaw to study engineering. Through other students at SVSU, he contracted me to teach his wife English. Over the weeks of dark-eyed Nada's instruction, he began sticking around to ask questions about life in the U.S.

One day when I arrived for Nada's lesson, dishes of food were on a cloth spread on the floor. After enjoying the delicious Middle East food, I thanked them profusely. Anwar wanted me to repeat his Arabic words which he said meant, "Thank you, God." Hearing Allah in his words, I gently explained I couldn't thank Allah for my food, because he is not my God. "My God is the Father of Jesus Christ."

Anwar was surprised. In his belief that there is only one God, he thought it was the same. With his permission, I began to explain how the Father sent His Son, Jesus. Anwar said God has no son, but Jesus is a prophet of God. I asked him, "Do you know that Jesus claimed to be the Son of God? How could He be a prophet from God, and lie by saying He is His Son? Either Jesus is a nobody, or He is Who He says He is, God's Son."

Apparently convinced, he changed the subject, saying Jesus was not crucified. "Really, he got away, and a bad guy got killed instead. I know Jesus didn't get killed, because God would never allow His Son to be killed. I am only a man, and I would not allow my son to be killed. So, you see, God would not allow Jesus to die on the cross."

"Anwar, this is precisely why God sent His Son to die on the cross, to show His love for you. He loves you so much, He sent His only Son to die a cruel death to set you free."

It was then that Anwar's face flew open, reeling in shock as his world rocked. I followed him to the couch. After composing himself, he continued to reason, "You must hate the Jews, because they killed Jesus."

"No, I don't hate the Jews. Jesus was a Jew. I love the Jews, because they brought my Messiah. Besides, it was the Romans who crucified Jesus."

"Then you must hate the Romans. Do you want to kill all the Romans?"

"No, I don't hate the Romans. You see, Jesus died for every nation. It was His plan of love to be the perfect sacrifice for all people everywhere. He shed His perfect blood, sent from the throne of Heaven to be spilled on the earth and offered on the altar of Heaven. He took up His life again and returned to Heaven. By this plan, all people are set free from sin. He invites all to be made pure by His blood sacrifice. There is only one thing to prevent someone from going to Heaven."

"What is that, Christine? Did Jesus die only for the Christians?"

"No, He died for the Muslims too. He loves Muslims. The only problem God has with anyone is the refusal of His sacrificial gift. Anyone who comes to Him saying, 'I appreciate the gift of Your Son. Thank You. I need Jesus' perfect sacrifice. Make me clean by the blood of Your Son.' Children born into Christian homes and countries must also do this. No one can take this great gift for granted. Each person must come to God through the sacrifice of His Son."

Anwar and Nada have returned to Saudi Arabia, and email between us has been censored by their government, but the seed of God's word has been planted in their hearts, and will bear fruit in season.

Jesus told him, "I am the Way-yes, and the Truth and the Life. No one can get to the Father except by means of me. If you had known who I am, then you would have known who my Father is." John 14:6&7 TLB

Thank You, Father, for the authority Jesus gave me to speak the truth in power. By Your grace, I will take every opportunity to do so!

AUTHORITY

© Christine List

ACROSS

1 Luke 5:24 that you may know that the Son of Man has authority on earth to forgive---

5 Luke 9:1He gave them power and --- to drive out all demons and to cure diseases

9 Luke 4:32 KJV And they were astonished at His doctrine: for His --- was with power.

11 1Chron.29:11 ---, O Lord, is the greatness and the power

13 Acts4:33 With great power he apostles continued to ---

14 Acts10:8 doing good and healing all who were under the power of the --

15 Eph.3:20 Now to Him Who is able to do immeasureably more than all we ask or --, according to His power that is at work within us,

16 Eph.1:19 and His ---great power for us who believe. That power is like the working of His mighty strength.

DOWN

1 Eph.3:18 may have power, together with all ---, to grasp how wide and long and high and deep is the love of Christ.

2 Acts 8:10 This man is the divine power known as the great power.

3 Acts 26:18 turn them from darkness to light, and from the power of ---to God

4 Acts1:8 you will receive ---when the Holy Spirit comes on you.

6 Luke 9:1 ---..gave them power to drive out all demons.

7 Mt.28:18 All authority in heaven and on --- has been given to Me.

8 2Chron.32:7 Do not be afraid..for there is a ---power with us.

10 Eph.1:21 far above all rule and athority, power and ---, and every title..

12 Eph.6:10 ---, be strong in the Lord and in His mighty power.

Solution on Page 77

PRAYER POWER

When Nada's husband asked me to teach English to her, I was sure God "set me up" to lead her to Him. It was up to me to discover how and when. My 20 year old Saudi student was pregnant with her first child. We had lessons in their small apartment.

Nada and I enjoyed our times together. She couldn't leave the apartment without her husband's permission, not even to walk outside with me. So, we visited and laughed inside. She introduced me to her mother on the computer. Mom asked me to help her daughter because she couldn't be with her. I promised I would any way I could.

One evening as Nada and I sat on the bed talking, she told me she was frightened of the pain of delivering her baby. When I offered to pray for her about it, she quickly accepted. I closed my eyes and surprised myself by asking Jesus to give her a painless delivery. No sooner than the words were out of my mouth, I thought, that's impossible. Now I'll make Him look bad asking for that.

When I opened my eyes, Nada sat there with her black eyes huge. Then she said in wonder, "I feel love! I never felt love before!" Jesus came to embrace her in His love, revealing Himself to her.

Some weeks later, Nada's doctor decided on a C-section, and Nada's baby, Noor (meaning Light) came into the world without pain. Jesus promised His disciples (me and you) "you will receive power when the Holy Spirit comes on you, and you will be My witnesses.."

Especially when praying for unbelievers, we can expect the supernatural, because the Lord wants to reveal Himself to them.

Ask, and you will be given what you ask for. Matthew 7:7 (TLB)

Father, I ask in the name of Jesus that Your Holy Spirit would give me power to witness and live the way You want. Help me remember that I'm not responsible to answer prayer; You are. Help me to ask big in faith.

PRAYER POWER

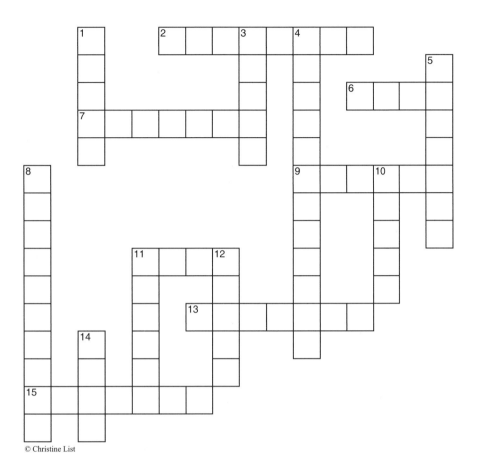

© Christine List

ACROSS

2 Luke 4:32 they were amazed at His --- because His message had authority

6 Prov 24:5 a --- man has great power

7 Eph 3:20 Now to Him Who is able to do immeasureably more than all we ask or --- according to His power that is at work within us.

9 Ps 68:35 God gives power and strength to His ---

11 Luke 5:24 that you may know that the Son of Man has authority on earth to forgive---

13 Eph 6:10 ---be strong in the Lord and in His mighty power.

15 Job 36:22 God is --- in His power

DOWN

1 Acts 10:38 doing good and healing all who were under the power of the ---

3 Is 40:10 the Sovereign Lord --- with power

4 Eph 1:19 and to His --- great power for us who believe. That power is like the working of His mighty strength.

5 1Cor 12:9 My grace is sufficient for you, for My power is made --- in weakness

8 Mt 22:29 you do not know the --- or the power of God

10 Acts 1:8 you will receive --- when the Holy Spirit comes on you

11 Zech 4:6 Not by might nor by power, but by My --- says the Lord

12 Ps 68:34 God, Whose power is in the ---

14 Luke 5:17 and the power of the Lord was present to --- the sick.

Solution on Page 77

PULLED FROM THE FLAMES

One balmy summer eve, I was on the phone with an internet technician. We waited for my slow old computer to reboot. Running out of chit-chat, I started cleaning my computer desk, a huge antique oak teacher's cast-off from some remodeled school. The built-in writing board creaked as I pulled it out.

Hiding in the back was a piece of paper. Curious, I recognized the Rodney Howard Brown salvation prayer script he gave us at an evangelism conference at TACF the day before 9/11. Just the week before, I'd thought of that script, and wondered where it was. I'd used the script many times, beginning with the dazed stewardesses sitting on the curb at our Canadian hotel on 9/11/2001, and taking it door-to-door in Saginaw.

I absently thought, "may as well read this to the tech while we wait." I started out, "M.J., do you know that God loves you, and has a beautiful plan for your life?" He fell right in, and said yes. So, I went along with the rest of the script, praying for him to know Jesus. When invited, he prayed for salvation.

It was so easy, I had to ask, "Well, what do you think of that?"

He happily answered, "The first thing I'm going to do when I get home is tell my grandma. This is a great day!"

I asked him if he would read his Bible. Excited, he said, "I'll read the Bible pulled from the fire!" He explained that when he was a baby, he was saved from the fire that destroyed his family's home. The only other thing saved from that fire was a Bible.

Can you see all of life as a "mission trip"? If so, then the nudges of the Holy Spirit will become more frequent and more easily heard, and eternal destinies can be changed because of your obedience.

2Tim 4:2 …*preach the Word of God urgently at all times, whenever you get the chance, in season and out, when it is convenient and when it is not…all the time be feeding them patiently with God's Word.* (TLB)

Father in Heaven, please help me to pay attention and use every opportunity to share the gospel of Jesus Christ. Open doors for me, that I may pull people from a future of eternal flames into Your loving presence forever.

PULLED FROM THE FLAMES

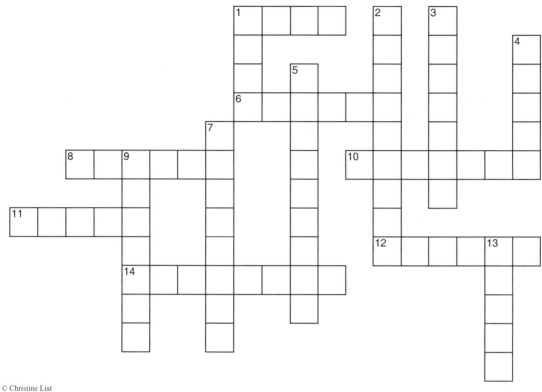

© Christine List

ACROSS

1 Luke 14:23 go..and --- them come in

6 Mt 18:9 ..--- into eternal fire.

8 Jude:7 ..an example of those who --- the punishment of eternal fire.

10 Mark 8:38 If anyone is --- of Me and My words...

11 Dan 12:3 those who lead many to righteousness will shine as the --- forever

12 Jude:23 --- others from the fire and save them

14 Acts 2:21 And --- who calls on the name of the Lord will be saved.

DOWN

1 Col 4:5 make the --- of every opportunity

2 Acts 1:8 and you will be My ----

3 Mt 25:41 ..into the ---fire prepared for the devil and his angels.

4 Ez 3:17 I will hold you accountable for his ---

5 Rom 10:14 how can they hear without someone --- to them?

7 2Tim 4:2 be --- in season and out of season

9 Mark 1:17 and I will make you --- of men

13 Mt 3:12 ..burning up the --- with unquenchable fire.

Solution on Page 78

FAITH

Two other women and I were cleaning an apartment. As I squirted Windex on the patio doors, a soft cry of pain came from the living room. I turned to see Lorie on the floor, one knee drawn up. Tearfully, the pretty petite brunette said to her daughter who regularly cleaned with her, "This is the same thing that happened to my other ankle. It popped when I tripped over the vacuum cord. I'm so sorry! I was trying to work fast. I can't get up."

My first impulse is to pray for anyone who's hurt. So I crouched on the floor next to her. I wanted to touch her ankle before praying, but I didn't want to risk hurting her more.

"Dear Jesus, please touch and heal Lorie's ankle." As I spoke, I realized I still had the Windex in my hand, and in the spirit, I saw myself spray the cleaner on her ankle!

Big Fat Greek Wedding came to mind and I felt silly. But I asked the Lord about it. It would be cooling, and He has a habit of asking people to use whatever is in their hands when a miracle is needed. Moses used a shepherd rod. Elijah, a mantle; Paul used the sweat band from his brow. So, I generously sprayed Lorie's ankle with window cleaner.

When the surprise left her face, the pain was gone too. Her face went blank, and then joyful as she exclaimed, "My ankle felt like it was on fire, and when you sprayed it, the fire went out! Thank You, Jesus!" She stood to her feet and continued cleaning.

Carrying the vacuum cleaner into the next house, she worked for 2 more hours, still exclaiming, "Thank You, Jesus!"

Matthew 9:29 *according to your faith be it unto you* KJV

Dear Lord Jesus, I put my faith in You. Help me to act in child-like faith so You can show Your love to me and those around me.

FAITH

© Christine List

ACROSS

3 Mk 6:6 He was amazed at their --- of faith

5 John 2:11 His disciples --- their faith in Him

6 2 Cor 5:7 we live by faith, not by ---

7 Acts 15:9 He purified their --- by faith

10 2 Cor 10:15 your faith continues to ---

13 Titus 1:2 faith and knowledge resting on the hope of --- life

15 Rom 11:20 you --- by faith

16 Luke 18:8 when the Son of man comes, will He --- faith on the earth?

DOWN

1 Mt 9:29 According to your --- will it be done to you.

2 Mt 21:21 if you have faith and do not ---

4 1Cor 2:5 that your faith might not rest on men's ---

8 Luke 7:50 your faith has --- you

9 Col 1:5 faith and love that spring from the --- that is stored up for you in Heaven

11 Mt 9:22 Your faith has --- you.

12 Jn 14:12 --- who has faith in Me will do what I have been doing

14 Gal 3:11 the righteous will --- by faith

Solution on Page 78

PATIENCE

When I was a little girl, I stood next to my dad at his workbench in the basement. All I could see besides Dad's legs were the rough 4x4 posts forming the legs of the table. They were fastened by long bolts with squares on the ends, and thick metal straps.

The bench was really strong, like my Daddy.

Occasionally in the summer, a tornado threatened. Then Mom took my brother and me under the workbench. Mom was sure if the house fell down around us, the bench would stand.

Dad took all things broken to the same bench. Dad's back was turned to me as he selected tools, wire, tape, screws, bits of wood… Usually the only tool I saw was the vise fastened to the edge of the massive table. I don't remember anything broken emerging unfixed from Dad's workbench.

As a young woman learning to trust God, I saw myself standing at my Father's side. I couldn't see what He was doing, but He turned to me with a smile, and then went back to work. I understood. He knows my need. He didn't forget me. When He's done, He'll give it to me. And it'll be fixed right.

I'm a big girl now, and determined to do it myself. I'd stayed in Mom and Dad's home since my marriage failed. Now since they died, and their house was sold, I had to find a place to live. I looked at houses for 2 years, knowing this day was coming. Three attempts to buy a house fell through when everyone said it's a buyer's market.

Two weeks before the deadline to get out of the house, I had no idea where I was going. God's answer to "what on earth is going on?" was to show me that I was firmly planted on the Potter's wheel. I looked at my options. How could I get off? I couldn't budge an inch any direction. I had no options, and was tempted to think that God was not involved and I'd just blown it. I refused to accept that thought, and decided to trust Him.

Then I realized the pressure all around me was relentless, unyielding Love. Father could have left me alone on the wheel, used some metal implement to hold me in place, like a mother propping her baby's bottle in the crib, instead of holding her child to her breast. The wall enclosing me is unmovable, but not rigid. It is God's hand I feel, Father's hand of Love. I kissed His fingers, pressing my face into His tender hand.

Acceptance and surrender to my Father's perfect love pleased Him and brought me into His complete peace. I didn't have a place to go yet, but I knew He was working on it.

Days later, His answer came, and it was better than any of the places I would have chosen for myself.

O Lord, You are our Father. We are the clay and You are the Potter. We are all formed by Your hand. Isaiah 64:8 TLB

Father, I'm thankful that You care enough to hold me to Your plan as long as I will stay. I choose You. I know You love me, and I want to see Your best.

PATIENCE

© Christine List

ACROSS

2 Ps 57:2 I cry out to God ..Who --- His purpose for me.

5 2Thes 3:3 the Lord is ---

7 Rom 8:25 we --- for it patiently.

9 Heb 3:4 God is the --- of everything.

11 Is 30:18 --- are all who wait for Him.

14 Prov 27:18 he that looks after his ---

16 Ps 62:1 My --- finds rest in God alone.

17 Ps 123:2 our --- look to the Lord our God

DOWN

1 Lam 3:26 it is good to wait --- for the salvation of the Lord.

3 1Thess 1:10 wait for His ---

4 James 1:4 Perseverance must --- its work so that you may be mature and complete

6 Jer 18:6 Like clay in the hand of the potter, so are you in My hand.

8 James 5:8 be patient and stand ---

10 James 5:10 as an --- of patience in the face of suffering

12 Gal 5:5 by faith we --- await

13 Phil 1:6 He Who began a --- work in you will ...

15 Is 64:4 Who --- on behalf of those who wait for Him.

Solution on Page 79

HIS PRESENCE, MY HOME

When I was a little girl, I stood next to my dad at his workbench in the basement. All I could see besides Dad's legs were the rough 4x4 posts forming the legs of the table. They were fastened by long bolts with squares on the ends, and thick metal straps.

The bench was really strong, like my Daddy.

Occasionally in the summer, a tornado threatened. Then Mom took my brother and me under the workbench. Mom was sure if the house fell down around us, the bench would stand.

Dad took all things broken to the same bench. Dad's back was turned to me as he selected tools, wire, tape, screws, bits of wood… Usually the only tool I saw was the vise fastened to the edge of the massive table. I don't remember anything broken emerging unfixed from Dad's workbench.

As a young woman learning to trust God, I saw myself standing at my Father's side. I couldn't see what He was doing, but He turned to me with a smile, and then went back to work. I understood. He knows my need. He didn't forget me. When He's done, He'll give it to me. And it'll be fixed right.

I'm a big girl now, and determined to do it myself. I'd stayed in Mom and Dad's home since my marriage failed. Now since they died, and their house was sold, I had to find a place to live. I looked at houses for 2 years, knowing this day was coming. Three attempts to buy a house fell through when everyone said it's a buyer's market.

Two weeks before the deadline to get out of the house, I had no idea where I was going. God's answer to "what on earth is going on?" was to show me that I was firmly planted on the Potter's wheel. I looked at my options. How could I get off? I couldn't budge an inch any direction. I had no options, and was tempted to think that God was not involved and I'd just blown it. I refused to accept that thought, and decided to trust Him.

Then I realized the pressure all around me was relentless, unyielding Love. Father could have left me alone on the wheel, used some metal implement to hold me in place, like a mother propping her baby's bottle in the crib, instead of holding her child to her breast. The wall enclosing me is unmovable, but not rigid. It is God's hand I feel, Father's hand of Love. I kissed His fingers, pressing my face into His tender hand.

Acceptance and surrender to my Father's perfect love pleased Him and brought me into His complete peace. I didn't have a place to go yet, but I knew He was working on it.

Days later, His answer came, and it was better than any of the places I would have chosen for myself.

O Lord, You are our Father. We are the clay and You are the Potter. We are all formed by Your hand. Isaiah 64:8 TLB

Father, I'm thankful that You care enough to hold me to Your plan as long as I will stay. I choose You. I know You love me, and I want to see Your best.

HIS PRESENCE, MY HOME

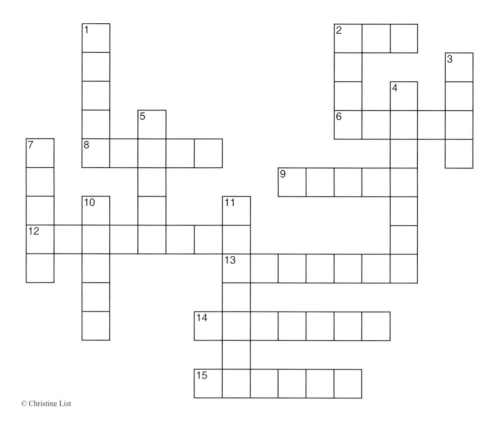

© Christine List

ACROSS

2 John 14:6 Jesus answered, "I am the ---"

6 Ps 119:168 all my ways are --- to You

8 Ps 23:6 I will dwell in the --- of the Lord forever

9 Luke 1:79 to shine on those living in darkness and in the shadow of death, to guide our feet into the path of ---

12 Ex 33:15 If your --- does not go with us, do not send us up from here.

13 Ps 31:20 in the --- of Your presence You hide them

14 Ps 73:24 You guide me with Your ---and afterward, You will take me into Glory

15 1John 3:19 we set our --- at rest in His presence

DOWN

1 Rom 1:17 The righteous will live by ---

2 Is 30:21 hear a voice behind you saying, 'This is the way; --- in it

3 Ps 73:23 You hold me by my right ---

4 Ps 41:12 You uphold me and set me in Your presence ---

5 Ps 48:14 He will be our --- even to the end

7 Prov 16:9 a man plans his course, but the Lord determines his ---

10 Acts 17:28 In Him we live and move and have our ---

11 Hosea 6:2 He will --- us, that we may live in His presence

Solution on Page 79

WALKING WITH THE KING

The hall I see in the spirit is enormous, ornately decorated in gold and brocade, with a 40 foot ceiling. It's full of people watching the huge entrance where the King and I stand looking in. He indicates to me with a smile that I'm to accompany Him through the tall arched door and into the international reception hall. I cringe, sure that my appearance will embarrass Him. I feel completely insignificant, the opposite of everything regal, as if I arrived by surprise in rags at a dress ball. His guests will surely notice that I am totally out of place, and I'll make Him look bad.

I love Him so much. He is everything to me, and all I want is to honor and love Him. I want to distance myself from His side, to watch with the others as He makes a perfect, grand entrance.

But as I look up to speak, He smiles at me, and says, "I love you. I chose you to walk at my side. I have made you altogether lovely. Place your hand on My arm, and walk with your King."

Suddenly unashamed, aware only of His royalty, I realize His beauty fills the room, and I am somehow covered in His perfection. People don't even see me, because when they look our way, they see only the radiance of the King.

God wants to assure you. The price Jesus paid was enough for you. When you arrive at the Ball, no one will be there to check your I.D. You are already known there.

Holy angels have sealed you. Heaven knows your name, and one day we will see as we are seen.

Isaiah 60:2&3 *the glory of the Lord will shine from you. All nations will come to your light; mighty kings will come to see the glory of the Lord upon you.* TLB

God in Heaven, I put my faith and confidence completely in what Jesus, Your Son, has done for me. I do not stand alone, but with Christ Jesus, my Husband and King. Thank You for Your wonderful plan to include me in the halls of Heaven.

WALKING WITH THE KING

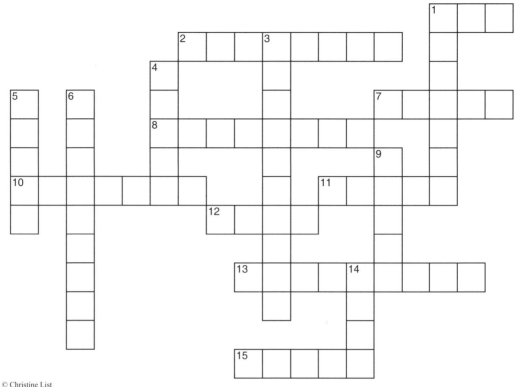

© Christine List

ACROSS

1 SS 8:6 Place me ...like a seal over your ---

2 Jn 6:27 On Him God has placed His seal of ---

7 Jn 10:14 I know My ---

8 Eph 1:13 Having ---, you were marked in Him with a seal

10 1Jn 3:19 God is --- than our hearts, and He knows everything

11 2Tim 2:19 the Lord --- those who are His

12 2Cor 1:21 it is God Who makes --- us and you stand firm in Christ

13 Rev 9:4 only those people who did not have the seal of God on their ---

15 1Cor 13:12 Then I shall know --- even as I am... known

DOWN

1 1Jn 3:2 when He --- we shall be like Him

3 Eph 4:30 with Whom you were sealed for the day of ---

4 2Tim 2:21 if a man cleanses himself...he willl be an instrument for --- purposes

5 1Cor 6:2 the saints will --- the world

6 2Cor 1:22 set His seal of --- on us

9 Jn 10:4 His sheep follow Him because they know His ---

14 1Pet 2:9 you are... a --- nation, a people belonging to God

Solution on Page 80

OCEAN OF LOVE
Solution

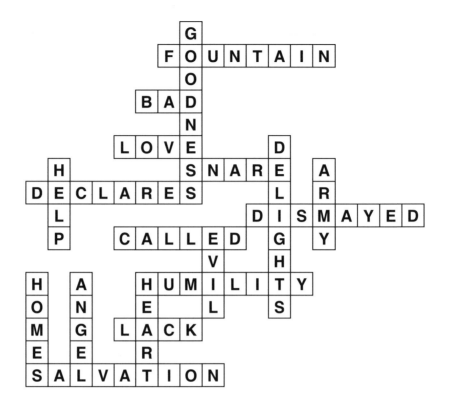

HARVEST
Solution

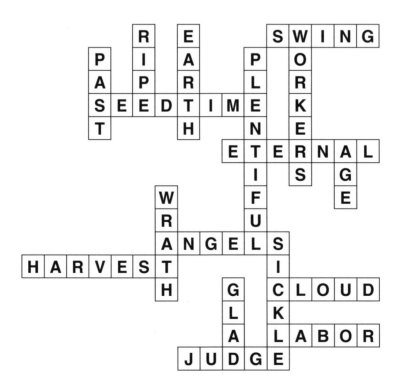

HEALED ON THE WAY
Solution

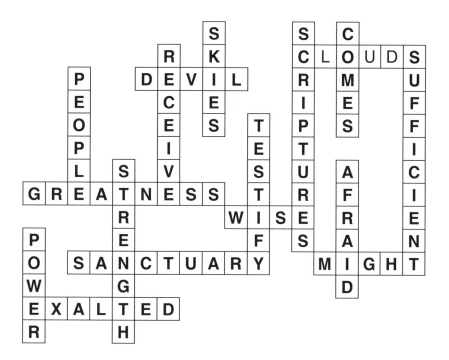

JOY IN OBEDIENCE
Solution

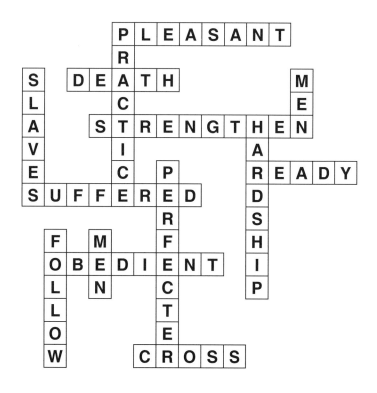

ARE YOU LISTENING?
Solution

TURN AROUND
Solution

OVER THE TOP
Solution

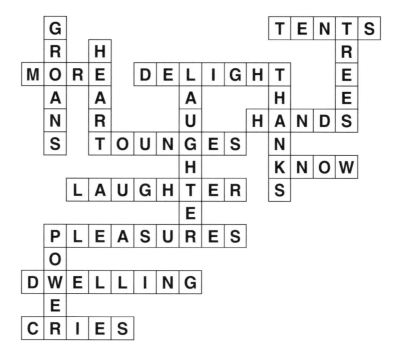

TEST OF FAITH
Solution

AND MY HOUSE
Solution

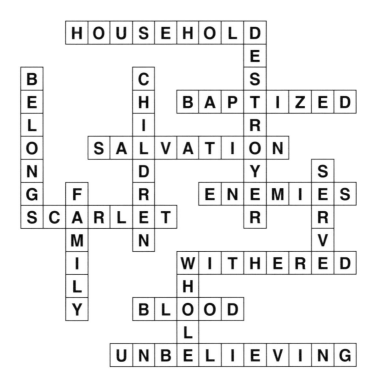

I AM GOD'S BELOVED
Solution

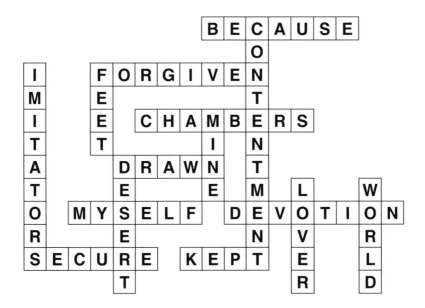

MORE THAN ENOUGH
Solution

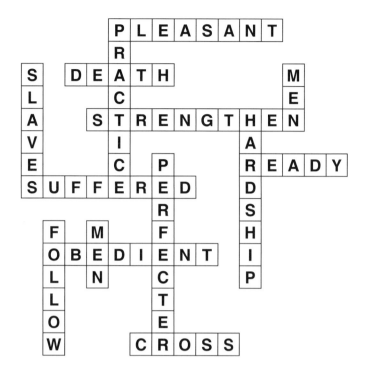

SAFE HIDING PLACE
Solution

TRUST AND OBEY
Solution

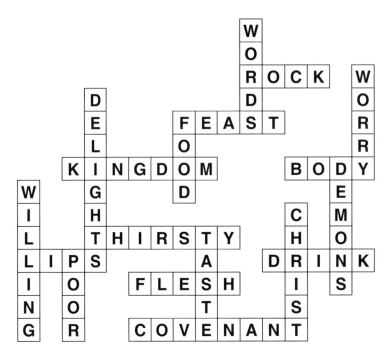

LOVE YOUR NEIGHBOR
Solution

HE RENEWS MY SOUL
Solution

EARLY MANSION
Solution

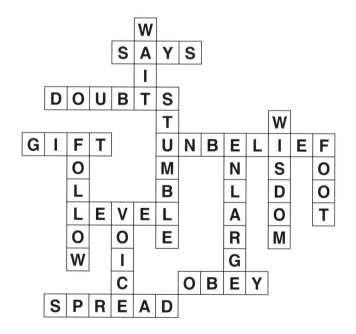

STICK TOGETHER
Solution

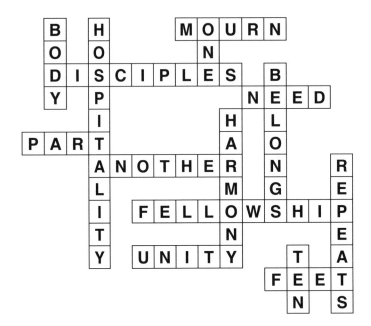

GLORY
Solution

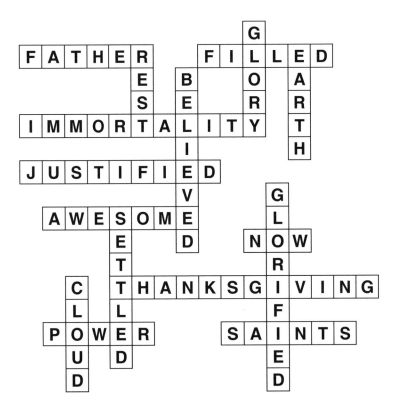

FAITHFUL SAVIOR
Solution

COMFORT
Solution

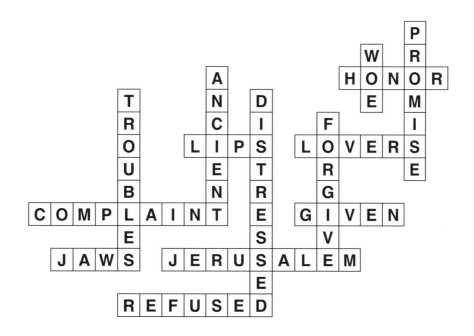

ANGELS IN THE MEADOW
Solution

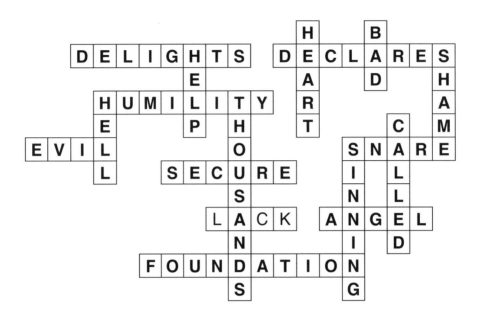

CHOOSE JOY
Solution

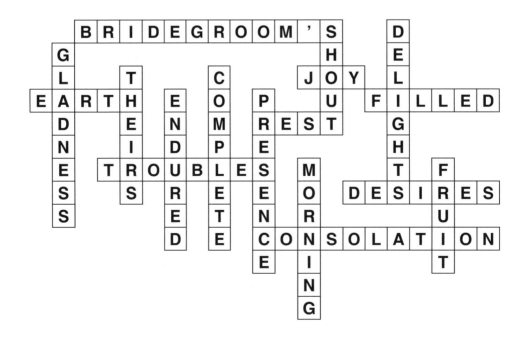

POWER OF FORGIVENESS
Solution

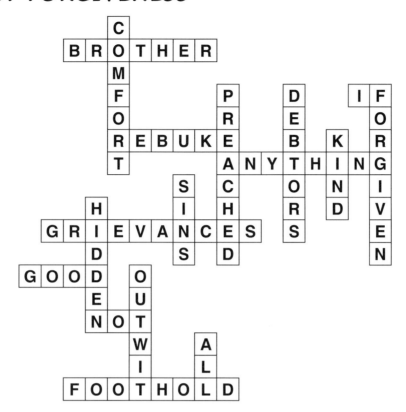

GUILT FREE
Solution

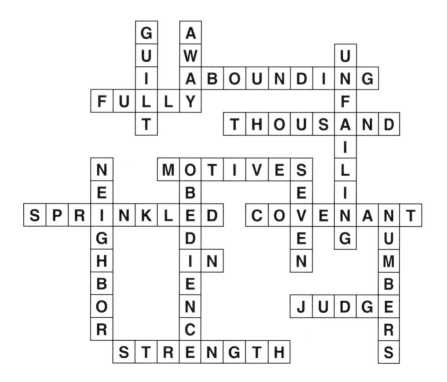

AUTHORITY
Solution

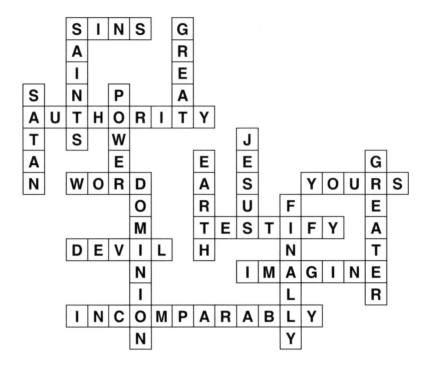

PRAYER POWER
Solution

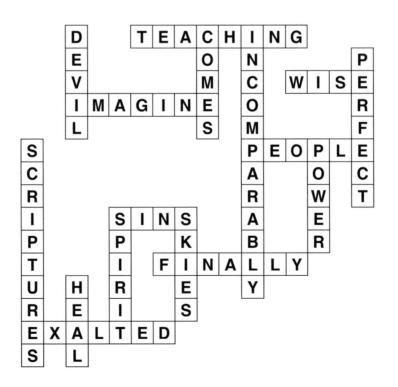

PULLED FROM THE FLAMES
Solution

FAITH
Solution

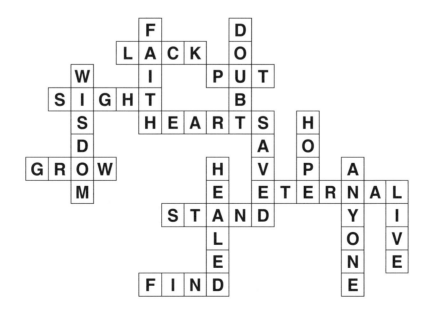

PATIENCE
Solution

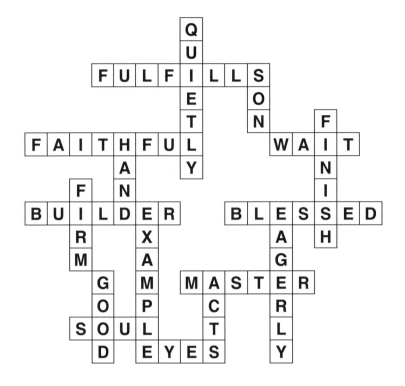

HIS PRESENCE, MY HOME
Solution

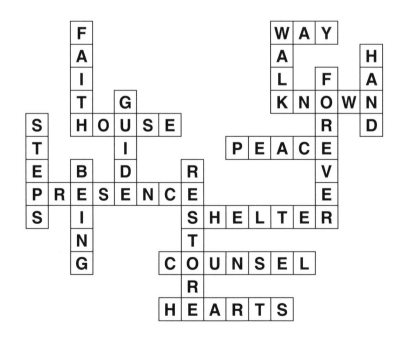

WALKING WITH THE KING
Solution

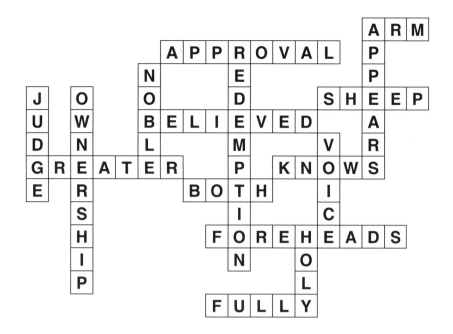